"The Burning Tree is a terrific debut. Thoughtful, engaging, spooky, disturbing in places, hopeful in others. A story of the damage carried by generations, and how that damage might one day be healed."

—A. LEE MARTINEZ, author of The Constance Verity trilogy

"Helen Dent's lyrical prose is hypnotic. You're not going to want to miss this stunning debut."

—LESLIE LUTZ, author of *Fractured Tide*, Junior Library Guild gold standard author

"Sparkling with witty prose and packed with complex relationships, Helen Dent's debut draws a timely picture of a world in which inherited prejudice has reduced a once-healthy community to self-interested tribalism. As we follow a tenacious and imperfect heroine in her race to save her sister, we readers are gently invited to wonder where our own points of view may be incomplete. Equal parts dystopia and modern fairy tale, *The Burning Tree* is not one to miss."

—HANNA C. HOWARD, author of *Our Divine Mischief* and *Ignite the Sun*

THE BURNING TREE

THE BURNING TREE

HELEN DENT

ENCLAVE

Escape

For Jonathan, always

one
day you
grasp my hand
as if we will leap out
beyond all these clouds
and branching stars and
meander our slow way
amid the many
limbed
sky

—Christine Switzer

IT WAS ALMOST A PERFECT AFTERNOON.

Even in Oakbend Woods, the sun struggled through half-bare branches, lighting up Drew's face when he turned to look at me. We tramped through thousands of brittle leaves, bound for the flat stones. For once I'd remembered my scarf, the red one with soft tassels, the one that made me feel like a picture of autumn from somewhere else. If I closed my eyes, I could imagine the scorched smell in the air was from hundreds of chimneys all going at once, not drifting from the center of the woods.

"Hey, Ellie, look," Drew said, stepping off the path and stooping under a knobbly tree. "Baby pine. You sketched these yet?" He rubbed a few needles between his fingers and handed them over, his palm brushing mine. Their bruised tang cut through the ash, and I breathed it in, reaching in my backpack for my notebook, loving the new branches with their hundreds of soft green spikes.

"Looks like you've got this patch down," Drew said, bending to look over my shoulder at the page filled with trunks and ivy, spotted mushrooms and pines. "We'll find a new spot tomorrow." But there weren't many places left in these woods I hadn't sketched. Except, of course, the center. As soon as I worked up the courage, that's where I'd go, though it would have to be alone. Even Drew would try to stop me from heading there.

His eyes were on me when I closed the notebook, and there was something in his gaze that set my heart hammering, though he didn't say another word. I slipped the needles into my pocket, and we ducked under the tree to the flat stones on the other side, two of them, like they'd been set there just for us. Like we were the only people left in the world and there was nothing outside this place. Drew leaned back against one of them, muscles taut, his sky-blue eyes fixed somewhere in the distance. All around us, the trees creaked a protest at being interrupted in whatever trees did when they were alone.

"Come back," I said, "from your million miles away."

He smiled his slow grin, and it melted me. I mean, I almost slid straight to the ground. "Guess I was somewhere else," he said. "Sorry."

"Take me there?"

He shrugged, picking at the sleeve of his navy pullover.

"Come on, Drew. That's the pact."

"Okay. All right." He leaned forward, put his hands on his knees, and took a breath. "It's just—I'm not sure how to ask this."

My heart stopped. Even the woods held their breath.

"So, I was thinking—maybe we could bring someone else in here. You know, so they could see what it's really like."

I jerked upright, the moment shattering. "You know we can't."

He sighed. "I'm not talking the whole town—just one person."

I stared at him, dread twisting my stomach. "Who?"

"Look, I know how things are for you sometimes." He didn't meet my gaze. "I thought—it might make it easier if—if you got to know her better. And if she got to know you."

The woods pressed in until I could hardly breathe through the stink of ash. Drew had seemed off the last few weeks, distracted, but so was everyone else with the tension rising in our town. I'd never imagined this. Not this. "You mean . . . Charlotte?"

He looked up, then nodded.

"You're kidding, right? Charlotte *Levy*?"

His hands tightened on his knees. "Yeah. But it doesn't have to be here. We could go—I don't know—wherever you want."

Charlotte was the last person I wanted to see in these woods or anywhere else, and he knew it. She'd turned on me in kindergarten and kept me out of every circle ever since, all the way to Bishop's Gap High. The girl looked like she didn't have a thought in her head except glossy hair and strappy shoes, but underneath, she was a snake. All week she'd been watching me with triumph under the usual disgust, and now I knew why. She'd taken Drew, just because she could. And he'd fallen for her, that was clear. Not me, her.

"Yeah, well, I already know her as well as I want to," I said, trying not to give myself away. "She's best in small doses."

He flinched. "Don't do this."

"I'm not the one who started it." My voice came out too high, on the verge of tears, and then anger swallowed everything else up, turning the sunlight red. "You realize, right, you have to choose? I'm Caster and she's Levy. You know that."

He stood, paced briefly in front of the rocks. "That's history. Ancient. Done." Like his words could stop the feud. Then he paused, turned to me. "You have to let it go. Ellie, you can't keep pushing people away."

I jumped up to face him. "It's not over, and it's not done. Not what the Levys did to us. Or what they still do. And the marks that come on people's doors? How do you explain that?"

He took my arm like he could fix everything just by being

there. "But you and Charlotte—you're just two people. Can't you see that?"

Drew was a Finch, which meant he'd never get a mark on his door, never have to march up to the Burning Tree in the middle of the woods. Finches could take any job they wanted, rise to judge or mayor, even. The only thing Casters had going for them in Bishop's Gap was the right to a Caster sheriff every other term. Grandad had won that for us in the last Unsettling. There'd been a truce since then, but that still didn't mean Drew could have us both.

When I shook my head, he laid his hand on mine, just for a second. He'd never done that before, and my heart turned over at his touch.

"I hope you'll change your mind," he said. "Because . . . I can't change mine."

I ran from the woods in a blur of tears, crossed the fields without seeing them. Once home, I stashed my sneakers under the porch, my wandering shoes that would give away where I'd been. Then I hurried through the kitchen, where Dad's oranges stood fresh and unspoiled in their patent-pending container, six weeks and still going strong, like the world hadn't just turned sick. Mom was at the stove, stirring her first-day-of-cold-weather pumpkin soup in the silver pot. "Good day, Ellie?"

"Sure."

I ran up the stairs before she could ask anything else, ripped off the scarf, stuffed it in the trash can, and spent the afternoon working through quadratic equations to keep from thinking about how Drew had just picked Charlotte over me.

Charlotte. *Levy.*

I kept tapping all the wrong numbers into the calculator while the walls closed in, but there was nowhere else to go. Not the abandoned Esso station where the other Casters massed before they headed out for dirt biking and messing around on go-carts. Certainly not the bougie malt shop the Levys haunted. Drew was probably there now too—with Charlotte. And I didn't belong anywhere but in the woods with him.

The calculator flashed *Error* for the thousandth time.

———

At supper in the yellow dining room where Mom's oil paintings lined the walls—sun-drenched visions of fields and bright flowers in a world without woods, without any trees at all—I couldn't eat a bite while my little sister Jean rattled on about some fort she was building with her friends.

Dad tensed. "Which friends?" Before Jean could answer, he looked to Mom. "Casters?" When she nodded, his shoulders relaxed.

Jean looked from face to face. "What's going on?"

For a second, the table went dead quiet. For my sister, the fairy-tale veneer hadn't yet rubbed off Bishop's Gap. She didn't see it for what it was—a place that should only exist in books, its own little pocket of insanity in the twenty-first century. Insanity with no cell reception.

Then Dad skewered a piece of roast beef. "Nothing, baby. We just have to be a little careful right now, that's all."

Mom put down her spoon. "What's happened, Jamie?"

He smiled, but the tension hadn't left his eyes. "Oh, nothing."

His unspoken *yet* hung in the air. We all knew the town was heating up, just like it always did when the mark came on someone's door. Two months ago, the mark appeared on a Levy house. Just a week later, it hit a Caster door. Now Levy deputies were pulling Casters over left and right, and Casters wouldn't buy from Levy stores. If nothing changed, we were heading straight for another Unsettling. And so, feuding hung in the back of everyone's mind, though there hadn't been a feud death here for a hundred years.

"They'll be looking to you," Mom said, and Dad answered like he always did.

"Let's hope it won't come to that."

Mom picked up her spoon again, stirring her bowl of soup like it was the only thing that mattered in the world. "We'll weather it. Always do."

"So, anyway," Jean went on, "we're going to paint the fort pink."

"Good for you," Mom said. Then she sliced apple cake and everyone went back to dinner as usual, except for me. I couldn't choke down a single bite. If the town blew up, Drew would be standing with the Levys now. With Charlotte.

I pushed my chair back, suddenly wanting to be anywhere else. Mom glanced at me. "Ellie, I haven't seen your sketches lately."

My sketches were leaves and vines and secrets. I kept my head down so she couldn't read my expression. "Oh, I've been busy, you know. Homework and . . ." my voice trailed off. If they knew I'd been going into the woods, sketching those woods, I'd be grounded for eternity.

Mom's gaze stayed on me a few seconds too long. When I finally looked up, worry flickered in her usually calm eyes.

After dinner, Dad snagged me in the hall. "Hey, you okay there, Els?"

I nodded.

"Want to help me open up those oranges, see what we got?"

"No, thanks."

He wavered like always when he wasn't sure what to say. "Well, if you change your mind, you know where to find me. And, hey, if you need 'em, I'm all ears."

But he wouldn't understand. Not about Drew or Charlotte, and certainly not about Oakbend Woods. We never talked about the woods. My parents just pretended it wasn't there, like silence could make it disappear.

And upstairs, there was nowhere to hide. Jean was in our room, scribbling in her journal, the one with poetry and scratch-and-sniff stickers. Her limericks always smelled like pizza.

She looked up, eyes bright with inspiration. "What rhymes with muffin, Ellie?"

"Shut up, Jean."

"Come on. You always know."

"I just don't want to do this right now, okay?"

Her eyes clouded. "What's wrong with you?"

I shot her a look. "You know, it doesn't matter anyway. No one wants to read what you write. You really don't matter that much, Jean."

As soon as I said the words, I ached to snatch them back. I don't even know why I said them, except I was losing Drew and Jean would never lose anyone. She danced through life like it was one of her poems. Now she flopped down on her bed as if I'd snatched the floor out from under her, pulling her unicorn bedspread over her head, which meant she wouldn't listen to another word. She tried to hide that she was crying herself to sleep, but her shaky eight-year-old sobs gave it away.

In the morning, the air outside hung thicker than I'd ever seen it, so ashy I couldn't even see our yard through the window. Something must have happened in the woods. I pushed away the stab of waking up to a world without Drew, slipped into the fraying pants I refused to outgrow, and tiptoed past Jean, who was still lying face down on her pillow. For a second, I considered waking her to apologize. But then she'd come after me, her hair a mess of tangles, clutching her ratty velvet squirrel. "Can I come, Ellie?" she'd say. "Can't I come?" And keep it up till she woke the house, which meant I wouldn't be able to get to the woods. It was forbidden to enter them except for the ceremony, let alone go all the way to the center. But Drew wouldn't keep me from the heart of the woods anymore, or my own fear, either. Nothing would.

I snuck outside, gasping for breath through the smoke, grabbed my red sneakers and my notebook from under the side porch and took off for the woods. Something was making the air worse this morning, so this might be my best shot at figuring out what the woods were hiding. For months, they'd been changing. I'd sketched the weirdness in my notebook when I was alone, patches of plants growing too large, swelling, sick. There had to be a reason, a connection to the Burning Tree at the center. I'd never shown those places to anyone, not even Drew, and I'd never mustered up the courage to go straight to the Tree. It haunted us, both Caster and Levy, kept our town stuck in the past, in the curse, while the rest of the world rocketed on.

But today, since nothing mattered anymore, the Burning Tree was exactly where I'd go. I ran down my worn path in the woods, refusing to look at the flat stones where Drew and I had been just yesterday. All this time I'd thought he saw through Charlotte. He'd certainly seen what she'd done to me. One day she and I were friends, sharing a kindergarten cubby, and the next she was shouting in the playground that I was a dirty Caster, that anyone who wanted to play with her couldn't talk with me or sit by me or get close enough to breathe my air. Kids stopped swinging to stare, or cackled from the jungle gym, and I ran into the woods so no one would see me cry. That was the first time I'd come in here. The trees wrapped their arms around me and never told my secret. That afternoon Drew found me, walked me home, and made me laugh until almost all the sting went out of *dirty Caster*. Almost.

People talked to me now—other Casters mostly, and some of the Finches who weren't in Charlotte's orbit—but I couldn't get myself to trust them, not after they'd turned on me so quickly for so long. And besides, until yesterday, I always had Drew.

Well, if he wanted Charlotte Levy, he could have her. I was good at alone.

When the path ended, I picked my way through fallen limbs and undergrowth to the clearing in the center where the Burning Tree stood, old and bent and scarred. Behind it, the Oakbend River raced by. Here it was really more of a creek, but it ran like it couldn't wait to get past, and no wonder. This ash tree was where it all started, the trouble between Levy and Caster, the curse the Levys had brought down on both our families.

I'd only been here for the ceremony, never by myself, and for a second, I couldn't breathe, like the Tree had closed its ancient branches around my throat. Its leaves rustled in a wind I couldn't feel, its branches flaming reddish in the smoky dawn light, and I was tempted to run when I saw the ivy. Just off the path, bloated leaves wound around a rotting stump. This was why I'd come, and I made myself stay, sketch everything I saw.

I forded the river on a rickety branch, and by the time I'd worked my way around the clearing, I'd sketched a pattern. The odd growth radiated out from the Burning Tree through the woods like spokes in a wheel.

Or an ancient eye, staring straight through me.

I took off for home without looking back, my lungs aching in the ashy air. I'd figure this out somewhere the Burning Tree wasn't looking over my shoulder. I only slowed down when I reached the fields behind our house. The kitchen curtains were open, so someone was awake, getting the Saturday pancakes started. I'd been gone much too long, and I was about to slip off my shoes, trying to think up an explanation for what I was doing outside in my socks at this hour of the morning, when I saw our door. I'd been in such a hurry when I left, I hadn't checked it.

A chill crept up through my legs and wormed its way right into my heart. Because there, in the bottom corner, a scorch in the shape of a crescent moon was seared deep into the wood. The shape we saw in our nightmares. The mark. On *our* door.

On the other side of it, my family were probably all gathered around the kitchen counter, Mom spooning pancake elephants with fantastical trunks onto the griddle for Jean while Dad boiled water for his banged-up French press, an old tin contraption that produced sludge only he could drink. But the coffee smell would shut out everything else, wrap them up in an island of being okay.

I wanted one more glimpse of them like that, before they knew about the mark. But when I pulled the door open, I was already too late.

2

INSIDE, OUR HOUSE SMELLED LIKE
the place had been burning for days, though—except for the mark
on the other side of the door—there was no sign of fire. Just plates
laid out on the oak table for breakfast, a pool of butter cooling on
the griddle, and a whisk trailing a Morse code of pancake batter
across the counter. Nothing else, as if everyone had vanished,
and I was the only one left in the world. And maybe that would
have been better.

"Jean." Dad's voice upstairs in our bedroom broke the silence.
"Come on, baby." Jean must have overslept, something she never
did for fear of missing out on a single second.

"Jeannette?" Mom was in there too, her voice shrill.
Something had pierced the bubble of calm that always floated
around her, which meant whatever the mark had done was in
that bedroom with Mom and Dad. And Jean. I would have run
up to them except it seemed every step took me further back, like
chasing a tide going out.

"We'll take the car," I heard Dad say as I finally stumbled up
the stairs. Mom ran past me, her fern-green eyes dark.

"Dad?" I called, desperate to hear assurance in his voice,
but he didn't answer. I made it to my bedroom door and then

I couldn't get myself to go farther. Jean lay on the bed like a withered stalk, unmoving, her curly, goldenrod hair the only bright thing about her. I could see all the veins in her small face. The velvet squirrel, the one she never let go of, lay crumpled on the rug.

Somehow seeing it lying there took me over the threshold just as Dad picked Jean up and rushed out. I followed them, clutching the stuffed animal like it would help somehow. *Wake up, Jean, please wake up.* I had to tell her I was sorry. Any second now she'd open her eyes and laugh at the joke she'd played on us. But when we reached the car, she was still limp.

Mom sat in the back with her. "Baby, just open your eyes for me," she pled over and over. "Squeeze my fingers, Jean, if you can hear me. It's going to be okay, baby, it's going to be all right."

I hardly heard her over the words playing in my head. *You really don't matter . . . you don't matter that much, Jean.*

That couldn't be the last thing I said to her. And I couldn't cry. I sat in the passenger seat with that stupid squirrel, watching Bishop's Gap fly by as houses gave way to the Esso station and County Grocers and the Meet and Three's diner.

At the hospital, a nurse I'd never met before took Jean's vitals. Then she took them again, tapped something onto a tablet, and gave us a starched smile.

"Dr. Finch will be in to see you soon."

Wisps of dull red hair had pulled free around Mom's face, and she patted Jean's veined arm rhythmically. "It's probably something to do with Jean's growth spurt. Or maybe she fell and didn't tell any of us."

Dad said, "Mm-hmm," and I grasped at the straw. Something must have happened before Jean came home last night. A fall at a friend's house while they built the fort, or something she'd eaten. Surely that's what the doctor would say.

"Come here, Ellie." Mom motioned me over, then held out her arms like she was looking to me for help. Her glance fell to the red sneakers I'd forgotten to take off, ragged edges of leaves from the woods still hanging all over them. My wandering shoes.

Her eyes went wide. She looked to Dad. "Jamie?"

He'd gone whiter than the hospital sheets. "Ellie, you know what we've told you."

Of course I knew. The woods were forbidden, but that was only because they held something we didn't understand. And my expression must have looked like I was about to fight back because Dad put his hand on my shoulder. "We're going to be talking about this, but right now's not the time. Let's keep it nice and cool in here." His voice stayed calm, but the circles under his eyes had deepened into half-moons.

Mom forced a smile and turned back to my sister to say brightly, "Jean, just as soon as you wake up, we'll all have pancakes." She tried to hide the fear in her voice, she really did, but when she smoothed Jean's sheets, her hands were shaking.

———————

I slumped in the green hospital chair, suffocating in the disinfectant smell, braiding and re-braiding my unbrushed hair. Raven wings, Jean called it. According to her, I also had sun-toasted skin and amber eyes of the clearest hue, though the mirror only showed me hair that wouldn't hang straight on a girl who'd outgrown herself.

Now I tried not to look at the veins branching out like roots across Jean's perfect face while Dr. Finch took forever to come.

The mark wasn't supposed to do things like this. When it hit the Levys' door two months ago, their pecan orchard shriveled up overnight. But Levys could afford to buy new land, replant. When it appeared on Sam Caster's door a week later, his family's well turned so bitter even the stock wouldn't drink it. County water came out, ran all kinds of tests, shook their heads. Like always when the mark came, there was nothing technically wrong, so nothing could be done. Sam's family spent the last of their money having another well dug. That one turned out worse. Now their place looked like a ghost house except with everyone still living in it. And Sam had stopped coming to school.

But the mark had never taken a person before. I squeezed the arms of my chair till my knuckles went white, making myself believe it wouldn't take Jean. Anything but her.

Still, I couldn't stop the panic rising in my throat. No one in Bishop's Gap knew how far the mark could go. We didn't even know how it reached our doors. Caster and Levy families used to wait up, straining to see something flesh and blood through the darkness, turn it away before it etched the mark. But then, fifty years ago, Celia Caster crouched behind her porch swing one night, a shotgun by her side. In the morning, her door bore the mark, her corn had rotted from the inside out, and she hadn't seen a soul.

The Burning Tree in the middle of the woods was behind it somehow. That's all we knew.

I didn't want to think about the Tree now, not with Jean's shallow breaths the only sound in the room, but still the images came flooding in. The stories Dad had told us. I hadn't let those pictures in for years, though I used to play them for hours on the unspoiled screen of my little kid mind.

Three families from up north—Caster, Levy, and Finch—had wandered these woods, the men in long beards, the women wearing flower-sprigged dresses, children scampering through the clear-aired forest. And it was all because the man leading the way, Benjamin Caster, the first of all the Casters here, had gotten his hands on Lewis and Clark's diaries and read them out to the others till they couldn't stand the walls around them anymore. The men were all for getting wagons and heading west, every man for himself, see who could go the farthest and dare the most, until Sylvia Caster and Elenora Levy set them straight. I could see those women sitting on horsehair sofas in their proper New England parlors, backlit by kerosene, laying down the law. *You will not drag us through the middle of nowhere with nothing to see but grass and sky till we go stark raving mad. And we won't be going alone. We head out together, somewhere there's trees, or we don't go at all.*

And that's why they went to Georgia, down to the dumping ground for outlaws and runaways. The third friend, Simon Finch, wrote in his records about that journey—*the Levys and Casters display a natural gift for friendship, an extraordinary inclination to mutual help*—which just showed how blind Finches could be. Eventually, they came to what Jeremiah Levy called *an auspicious valley in the ridge, arranged to great advantage around a tree that holds up the sky.* The Tree was so tall then, they couldn't see its crown. Even in summer, its leaves shone golden in the sun. Then the old injury. The curse.

A rap sounded on the hospital door. Dr. Finch swept in with the nurse right behind him and picked up Jean's chart. Mom fumbled for my hand. "Well, what do we have here?" He slipped on black-rimmed glasses and scanned the notes. "Uh-huh."

His voice was cheerful enough, but before he turned to Jean, his glance ran over my parents' faces, intent. He took Jean's pulse again, opened her eyelids and flicked on his flashlight.

Then he handed the flashlight to the nurse. "Check that for me."

She peered into my sister's eyes. "I see it," she said.

"See what?" said Mom, her voice tense.

"Dilating just like normal," the doctor replied, grinning at a spot on the wall past all of us.

He reached into a drawer under the bed and pulled out a reflex hammer. I wasn't fond of how that thing made me do something I hadn't chosen. Jean had always flinched away too, before today. Dr. Finch aimed and struck. Under her purple, sparkle pajamas, Jean's leg kicked.

"Uh-huh," he said again, but he swallowed hard. "I have to tell you, I don't like the look of those veins. We'll go ahead and run more tests, of course, because on the face of it . . ." I knew what he was going to say next. My stomach twisted as Mom's hand slipped from mine. "On the face of it, she's not presenting with the symptoms I would expect from her current condition."

Dr. Finch had delivered both of us. Maybe that's why, after the nurse left, he lost his bedside manner and became just another person in the group standing around my sister. Dad took Jean's hand and reached out another for Mom's, but she was so obviously in a place all by herself now that his hand drifted to his side again.

"Should I make the calls?" Mom said when the doctor had pulled the beige hospital curtain around us and retreated. "Or wait till the tests?"

In the silence that followed, I crept up and set the velvet squirrel I'd forgotten I was still holding onto the crook of Jean's arm.

"We should wait," Dad finally said.

Mom bit her lip. "But we've seen it. We know what this is."

"The mark," I whispered, counting the steps to the bathroom where I could be sick.

———

The next day, when all the tests came back normal, Mom picked up the phone. "It's Arden," she said again and again in the room where Jean lay, small and silent. "It's time."

3

THAT AFTERNOON, WE DROVE TO
Oakbend Woods for the ceremony. Since the hospital couldn't
help Jean, this was her last chance to come back to us. With
every breath, I'd become just one word in and one word out.
Please.

The trees looked on, shrouded in October mist, as Dad
pulled up in the gravel lot and the parking brake screeched
through the car. The others had already come. Pickups fanned
out around the lot, punctuated by the occasional sedan. Casters
poured out of them, dozens of Casters. Next to us, Great-Aunt
Ruby slammed the door of her ancient Buick, then jerked back,
caught by her fringed shawl. She always wore that thing, swept
around town in it, knocking over flowerpots and small dogs.
For a second, I looked over to Jean to share the laugh and then,
seeing her empty seat, I remembered for the hundredth time
why we were here. It must have been shock that kept shutting
my brain down like that, or because no one was talking about
it—like if we stopped pretending everything was okay, we'd never
break Jean's spell.

Grandad eased himself from his rusted Chevy, his face set

like the cliffs they'd dynamited around Bishop's Gap to build the road. But the grief still showed through, breaking me even more.

"All right," declared Mom, "this is it. You have the matches?"

Dad nodded, patted his red flannel pocket. "I do. And the lighter, just in case."

I handed Jean's stuffed animal to Dad and our family led the way to the woods. We weren't taking the ferny trail, my way in. This was the official entrance, the wide path, the mouth that led to the Burning Tree. Just before I reached it, someone caught my sleeve, someone who wasn't a Caster.

Drew.

"You're not supposed to be here," I hissed, hating how the sight of his stupid familiar blue-and-white striped polo made me want to dissolve. Scream. Take an ax to the woods for Jean.

"I know," he whispered, walking along with me against Caster glares. "I'm—you know, I'm really sorry about your sister. And I've—I've missed you."

"Yeah, okay," I said, and then I let the momentum of the crowd push me forward and away from him. He'd made his choice. You can't be friends with a Caster and in love with a Levy. It just doesn't work. Between friendship and love, when it comes right down to it, it's obvious which will win. Plus, if I'd stayed another second, I would have thrown myself at him, blubbered into his crisp notebook paper scent. And I couldn't stop. I had to do this right for Jean.

Inside, the woods arched up into a tangled roof. All the members of my family tree walked along just like normal. If normal was a parade through the woods with russet leaves crunching underfoot. And we wore jeans, not robes—except, of course, for Aunt Ruby's shawl. Somehow this made everything worse, like the ceremony wasn't just something from a sidebar in my anthropology textbook on ancient myths and rituals. Casters and Levys had been making this march for over a hundred years, ever since the first mark on the first door left a burning smell like the one that hung around the Tree in the center of the woods. They'd known the Tree was angry, and they'd brought whatever they could think of to appease it. No one spoke of those first sacrifices. Now we offered symbols, tokens of loss. I glanced at the stuffed animal in Dad's hand, its head hanging limp.

When I'd come down this path before, I'd thought this ceremony was all empty effort, some instinct people had to do something when there was nothing to be done. But they said that once this ritual had worked, and now I clung to the possibility as I pictured the veins standing out under the papery skin of Jean's face. Mom put her arm around my shoulders, and I grabbed Dad's hand, something I hadn't done for years, like linking might help. We walked together through squares I'd mapped and mapped again. Just out of sight, leaves were growing too large for this climate, the secret only I knew.

If I'd brought Jean in to see them, she'd have laughed, then gathered them into a pile like the one we raked each year in Grandad's yard to slide down till it was time for the bonfire and roasted marshmallows. Jean always crammed her stick full and burned all the marshmallows to a crisp. Afterward, she'd fall asleep on the five-minute drive home, her face beaming and sticky. In a week or two from now, we'd do that again, and she'd be there for it.

She had to be.

When we reached the clearing where the Burning Tree stood, all the footsteps stopped. In the silence, dry leaves clicked against each other, crackled, and seemed to spark in the muted sunlight. The suffocating echo of my heartbeat closed my throat. Just a few steps away, the Tree seemed to warn me back. I shook the feeling off and stood my ground, fixing my gaze on the river running behind it.

Dad let go of my hand, ran his fingers down Mom's face, and stepped to the tree. He set Jean's velvet stuffed animal at the base of its trunk, then held up the matches. "For Jean," he said.

"For Jean," we answered.

Then he struck a match on the bark, etching Jean's initials deep into the tree till the air reeked of sparks, recording our loss, pleading for mercy. We could still read other initials, the recent ones. The rest, both Levy and Caster, dozens of them by now, had been swallowed by the tree's rings.

Finally, Dad turned, sweat trickling down his face, and if anything could give my sister this one-in-a-thousand chance, it was the look in his eyes. "For Jean," I whispered.

———

Dad stopped at the first payphone past the woods. From the way his shoulders slumped, I knew even before he turned around that the ceremony hadn't worked. Nothing had changed for my sister. After that, I couldn't put a single thought together as the car took us along, and when we returned to the hospital, I refused to get out of the car. Actually, it was more like my legs wouldn't move.

"Ellie," Mom said, turning to look at me, "I know this is hard, but Jean needs to hear our voices. She'll follow them back."

I couldn't believe she was still spinning that make-believe world. "No, Mom, she can't. She's gone. That *thing* took her."

Mom flinched like I'd slapped her. I couldn't understand what was wrong with me, the acid words that kept spilling out of my mouth, first with Jean, now here, so I gripped the torn fabric of the seat where we'd tried to stuff two bicycles in one too many times and turned on Dad.

"Why did you keep us here?" I accused, voice raised. "You could have taken us anywhere else. And then Jean would be okay."

His face froze.

Mom's gaze bore into mine. "Let's get one thing clear. We will not turn on each other." She unbuckled her seatbelt. "And no one's giving up on Jean."

More than anything, I wanted it to be that simple.

Dad's smile was working again, and he offered it to me. "Tell you what, Ellie. We need something in our stomachs, no matter what."

He turned to Mom. "You go on in with Jean, Arden. We'll bring you a plate."

"Jean will be okay. She'll be fine. It will probably just take a while," Mom said, and then marched away before anyone could negate her last word.

Dad put the truck into gear, and I sat, rigid. Nothing he could say would make this better, especially his usual stale line that things had a way of working out. Though, deep down, I still wanted to hear those words. Just for a moment, I wanted to pretend like everyone else.

We rode to Main Street in silence. I used to love downtown, ducking into the bakery for gingerbread men, dodging past the empty storefront everyone still called the old five and dime. They said that place was haunted, but when Jean and I had swapped rumors, Dad just shook his head. "The people who own it, they aren't from around here. They can't figure out how to make a go of anything." The look on his face meant the conversation was over, but it was all part of Bishop's Gap, part of home.

Now I could only see the paint peeling off the buildings faster than anyone could brush it on, our bitter air worming its way into everything. And, in the rearview mirror, a Levy deputy tailing us. Dad's knuckles were white as he pulled in front of Meet and Three's, but he didn't even glance over as the deputy slid past. "Eyes front, Els," he said, and I stared at the scratched-up glove compartment till it hit me. The mark on our door hadn't just taken Jean. It was about to push this town right over the edge.

As soon as the patrol car turned out of sight, Dad said "Shall we?" like nothing had happened, and we walked into Meet and Three's where red checkered curtains decked every window and red checkered napkins sat on every table like this was a normal diner in a normal town. They even painted the front once a month, sometimes twice, to keep up the illusion.

We walked past the late lunch crowd to our usual booth. Before he sat down, Dad glanced at the door. The patrol car hadn't circled back, but that didn't mean it wasn't out there, waiting just past the sea of checkered tablecloths. I couldn't get my thoughts together anymore, couldn't think of a single thing to say, so Dad ordered chicken fried steak and okra for himself, and a burger, fries and chocolate float for me, which seemed massively inappropriate. Burgers and fries were for birthdays and the last day of school, not the end of the world.

Then he kept wrapping and unwrapping his fork in its little paper napkin while I watched drops of condensation mass on my ice water, slip, and mass again. Something about that pattern seemed familiar. I clutched at it, but it melted away through the sludge of my thoughts.

Dad cleared his throat, and I stared across the table at him, at the lines on his forehead, the circles under his eyes. *Everything's going to be fine*, he was about to say. Except he didn't. "Here's the thing, Ellie. I've been lots of other places." He was shredding the napkin now into little flecks of nothing. "And they're just like here."

My words finally jolted free. "People's doors get scorch marks everywhere you go?"

"No, of course not. But things happen to them, same as they do here."

"Not having the mark seems better," I said. I'd seen them leave, the people who wanted to retire somewhere quaint or the ones who noticed our town had only one restaurant and so was ripe for opportunity. They always watched their mirrors on their way out, their faces white.

Millie Finch slid a burger in a poppyseed roll under my nose, and the greasy smell of fries turned my stomach.

"True," Dad said when she'd gone. "I understand, I do. I thought so too—that other places would offer more." He seemed to know what I'd been thinking. "I couldn't wait to get out of this town. And I did try it for a while before I came back and married Mom, you know that. But," he hesitated, "how can I explain this?"

He drowned his okra in ketchup, mind clearly elsewhere. "Here, people see the way the world really is. Bad things happen everywhere, and I wish I could change that for you. But you have no idea how exhausting it is to live where people keep closing their eyes to that." He looked straight at me, his gaze so intense I couldn't glance away. "I see myself in you, Ellie, always have. I see the way you want to fix this world. But some things can't be mended. Learn that now, and you'll save yourself a lifetime of regret." Then he tried to smile, like just saying the words had been enough. "For better or worse, we're tied to this place."

"You mean we can't get away." I hadn't meant to talk so loud, but even the Levy side of the diner fell silent. By the time sounds started up again, ice clinking in glasses, forks scraping against plates, I couldn't look at my fries or the squishy center of the tomato slices a second longer. "I don't feel good." I stood. "I've got to go."

"Ellie," Dad called after me, but the jangling door closed on his voice.

Outside, I took off past the empty storefront without a second glance and ran all the way home, with *no way to help Jean* pounding through my brain. Maybe Dad was right, and the world was so crammed full of sadness it had no room for anything else. I scrambled into my old hiding spot way under our side porch like I was six again, breathed in its familiar musty smell until I could think straight.

The pattern of condensation that had slipped down the glass back at the diner hung in my mind, and I scratched its shape into the dirt with a twig, scattering roly-polies in all directions. Lines connecting into one, like something I'd seen before. Like the veins on Jean's face.

And something else.

Roots.

I sat up, banging my head on the spiderwebbed boards. Then I grabbed my notebook from its hiding place, ripped out every page I'd sketched in the woods, and laid them out on the dirt with the Burning Tree in the center.

There it was, the answer I'd been searching for. All the lines of odd growth started in the middle, then branched out through the woods. I was looking at the reach of the Burning Tree, its roots spreading just below the surface. And roots keep going until something stops them, which meant it was under our house. Under all our houses.

I gripped the twig so tight it snapped in my hand. Over the years, people in Bishop's Gap had tried all kinds of things to break the curse. Charms, incantations, even exorcisms—but always at a distance, from outside the ring of the woods, only daring to go into Oakbend for the ceremony and then leaving as fast as they came. They never breathed a word about the Tree outside Bishop's Gap, didn't even speak of it to each other except whispers in secret, afraid of what they didn't know, terrified they'd make everything worse. So, no one had seen what I'd mapped, the span of the Burning Tree. They didn't know its roots had already come to us, marking our doors just like it scorched the air. That's what was killing Jean.

I placed the pages back into my notebook, my heart pounding. Dad had it wrong. There was something I could do. If I destroyed the Tree, the curse would die with it, so there was still a chance to save my sister. But even if I managed to cut it down somehow, that wouldn't fix anything, not right away, not in time. Roots could spread their poison long after the trunk was gone. And there was only one way to get at the roots that I knew of. I'd learned it from Grandad when he cleared brush from his fields.

I needed to go into the woods, straight to the Burning Tree's gaze. And then, just as soon as I figured out how, I had to burn it down.

4

IN CASE DAD WAS STILL LOOKING for me, I ducked through fields all the way back to town. On Main Street, his truck was nowhere in sight, but the patrol car continued to circle, so I kept to alleyways until I reached the Bishop's Gap library and dashed inside, closing the tall door safely behind me.

But then all I could find about burning down trees was how *not* to do it—keeping lit cigarettes out of dry brush, quenching campfires before you leave, that kind of Smokey Bear thing. I could see Smokey now, pointing a finger at me, the only one who could prevent forest fires.

In particular, the one I was planning to set.

For a second, he made me question my strategy. I gazed out the familiar corner window where the gray line of the trees hung in one direction, and the brick wall of the bakery filled the other. This was the best spot in town, the only place the ash smell couldn't reach. I could almost taste sugar crystals in the air. And no one else knew about it. No one came back here, in the corner behind the encyclopedias that didn't belong to Levy or Caster. Which made it the ideal hiding place when the other spaces got too small, or too grubby, or Jean discovered them and filled them with stuffed animals. I used to lose myself at this table for hours, reading how to tell a bryophyte from an embryophyte. Plants that flourished in temperate climates. Plants that flourished in tropical climates. Plants that flourished where roots burned like veins under the ground.

And that, after all, was the point. All I wanted to do was get rid of one rotten tree and its root system. Even Smokey would understand this exception—especially if he'd seen my sister.

I cracked open another forestry book, one that had my name, and only my name, on the due date card. Twice. One in careful block letters and the other an awkward cursive where I'd made all the loops hearts, back when I'd thought the world was a different kind of place. Now the second chapter took me so deep into "Disturbed Habitats: Abnormal Outcomes" that I didn't hear the librarian, Miss Prow, till she tapped me on the arm. I started, shutting the book with a dusty bang. She looked down at me with her kind blue eyes, faded from a life of nothing but reading.

"You got a research project there, Ellie?"

I nodded. I hated to lie to Miss Prow, who'd introduced me to John Muir and John James Audubon and who let me come through the door marked "Staff" on cold days for hot chocolate. But strictly speaking, research was exactly what I was here to do.

She set an arthritic hand on my shoulder. "I can't fathom that. What are they thinking, giving you an assignment at a time like this?" The hand tightened to a claw around my collarbone. "I guess the world never does stop spinning. Probably best or we'd all have snapped the whip off it a long time ago."

That made no sense. She was looking over my head, her dull eyes glazed. My stomach, which had settled down some in this usual corner, wrenched again. Was she losing her mind right here, alone with me? Then she sniffed in the way people do when they've decided that, though they'd like to cry, they shouldn't. In some roundabout way, this was about Jean, though Miss Prow was being nice enough not to say so. And really, what was there to say besides, *Sorry your life just ended*?

She released my shoulder and pointed a bent finger in the direction of the historical fiction section.

"When you're ready for a break, let me know. I've squirreled away a box of windmill cookies from next door."

Miss Prow never offered cookies. Crumbs in the library were her one fixation.

"Thanks," I said, and she turned, tapping a steady rhythm across the floor with her sensible black shoes, her gray skirt swaying in time. She wasn't a Levy or a Caster, not even a second cousin by marriage. Like a handful of other families in town, some Prow ancestor had married into the Finches and, against all odds, decided to stay. And just for a second before she disappeared back into the stacks, she seemed more substantial than any of us, though I didn't have the time to wonder why. Any minute now Dad would think of this place and come looking. I whipped open the two remaining books to their back pages, stabbed at one, and ran my finger down its index. I didn't have far to go. Because right between "composting" and "copper leaves, causes," there it was in black and white.

controlled burns

I hurried home through the ash-glow twilight to change into my best guess at flame resistant clothes and my red shoes for luck. On the kitchen counter, the oranges still sat perfect and unchanged. But upstairs, Jean's half of our room was already fossilizing, her crayoned unicorn pictures on the wall like something from a museum. I tried not to look at all those green and pink outlines, keeping my mind on what I had to do. Because if I made a mistake, if the underbrush caught, there were houses near the woods. I pictured flames ripping through roofs, eating up dry fields. But I couldn't think of that, and I clutched at phrases from my research— *restoration of the ecosystem, prevention of catastrophic fires*—muttering them over and over till I could breathe again. I was preventing catastrophe. Restoring Jean.

And then, right before I pulled on my sneakers, the worst happened. The back door banged open, and Dad called, "Ellie?"

I had just enough time to stuff the shoes under the bed before he came in. When I looked up, the circles under his eyes had taken over.

"Els, where have you been?"

I dodged. "How's Jean?"

"Well, she's—she's holding her own. About the same, the doctors say."

His glance flitted around the room, landing everywhere but on me. He didn't believe a word he was saying, and if I hadn't had a plan to fix this, to save her, I would have been terrified. She'd slip away with my words still hanging between us.

"Your mom doesn't want to leave Jean's room, you know, and I really should be there too."

"Okay," I said.

"So, you'll be staying with Grandad a few days."

"Okay," I said again, trying not to let excitement leak into my voice. Grandad had sold most of his farm, but his barn was still full of all the supplies I'd need. Ignition at my fingertips, with no reason for anyone to ask questions about why I was poking around.

On our way over to his house, as the setting sun blazed through the windshield, Dad shifted in his seat. "Look, I shouldn't have to say this, but I will."

This was the thin ice part. I could hear it in his voice. My sneakers were burning a hole through my overnight bag, and my heart pounded so loud above the rumble of the engine I was sure he could hear it.

"You've been going into the woods, we know that," he said, maneuvering around a deep pothole. "I could just forbid you to go back, but we've been down that road, haven't we?" He looked over at me, and I nodded, keeping my eyes on the glove compartment. He was about to make me promise the impossible, that I'd stay away, and I couldn't lie straight to his face.

Then he sighed. "This town is a balancing act. We're all just stepping through a dance we hope won't get anyone killed." Without warning, he pulled over to the side of the road, stopping right by a yellowing tree Jean and I used to climb for its perfect foothold branches. "Ellie, you know the history here," he said, turning to face me, "but that's different than having a gun cocked in your face. You understand me?"

I nodded again, still staring at the three little scratches by the glove compartment handle. "I keep my head down, Dad."

"Good. I know you do. And see, it's the same with the forest.

Except there, nobody knows the steps of the dance." I did look at him then, at his graying face. "So, we stay away. *You* stay away."

I smiled, hoping that would be enough. But of course it wasn't. "Promise me, Ellie."

The answer clicked, and I looked him right in the eye. "I promise I won't go wandering." And I wouldn't. Not a single meander. Just straight to the Tree and back.

Dad let out his breath. "Good," he said, putting the truck into gear.

Now I just had to get past Grandad.

5

WHEN WE PULLED UP GRANDAD'S old gravel drive, the screen door banged open, and he shot out.

"No change," Dad called.

Grandad shook his head. He looked suddenly ancient, more stooped than I'd ever seen him. But he'd be back to normal, too, just as soon as I could get to the woods.

Dad brushed a kiss on my cheek. Then, right before he pulled out, he rolled down the window. "Oh, and Ellie knows, she's to stay inside for the time being. School and this house only." He couldn't have chosen a worse time to mention that.

Grandad nodded. "Getting bad out there?"

"Whole place is on edge."

All except Jean. She was slipping off it. I wanted to grab my shoes and make a dash for the trees then and there, but with Dad's eyes fixed on me, I turned and followed Grandad's slow shuffle inside.

He walked down the dark hall to the kitchen without bothering to turn on the light. "How about a bite to eat?"

"No, thanks. I'm not really hungry."

"Well, I don't figure anybody is, but we can't go keeling over, make more bother."

I felt around in my bag for my sneakers. "Could I just go out a minute before supper, walk around a little, you know, stretch my legs?"

Grandad shot me a sharp look over his plaid shoulder. "You heard your daddy."

I'd have to wait for a moment of distraction, though that didn't seem likely anytime soon. He'd never been so slow to get two plates of food together, shuffling from the fridge to the counter and back again in his kitchen that always smelled like dust and garden plants. He gathered tuna fish, sliced tomatoes, lettuce, relish, and everything else he could find on the shelves that would fit on two slices of wheat bread. And all the time, Jean was maybe getting worse, slipping away so far she could never come back. When fidgeting got the best of me and I tried to help, he waved me away.

"Take a load off," he said. "You've been going through a lot."

He picked up an orange and, for a second, I thought he was going to slice that up and put it on the sandwich too. But he cut a hole into it, snipped off the end of a straw, stuck that in, and handed it over like I was three. I didn't want to sit there in a plastic bucket chair drinking from an orange and counting the tiles on the ceiling, but Grandad wasn't whistling like he always did, which meant nothing was under discussion, so I hunkered down and drained that orange dry.

After dinner, which we ate on brown trays in the den watching the news—distant disasters that suddenly seemed way too close—Grandad squirted lemon dishwashing liquid into the sink and watched the bubbles rise without a word. I dried the dishes so fast most of them sat wet on the shelves. When I finished, Grandad stepped out to the den. From there, he couldn't see the front door.

"You know what we need?" he called as I was about to make a break for it. "A round of checkers." And just like that, he'd reeled me back in. We sat at the table where he'd taught me to play, and I maneuvered straight into a double jump to get it over with. Grandad raised an eyebrow.

"Your mind on something else there, Ellie?"

I shook my head, glancing at the door, and he slid a piece forward. Once I got outside, ten minutes tops and I'd be in the woods.

"Because it'd be in the realm of imagining you might be wandering a little," he went on, tapping the checkers he'd captured on the table. "Or planning to wander, and I'm not going to let you do that, you hear? We're in deep waters right now. I've seen this before."

My stomach clenched. Grandad never talked about the past. How during the last Unsettling all the families in Bishop's Gap were priming their shotguns before he got the Casters to stand down, negotiated a peace. But he wouldn't be able to fix our town a second time. And Dad wouldn't either because every Caster here knew even peace hadn't made things fair.

Grandad was thinking the same thing, maybe, because his face hardened. "Ellie, listen to me now. The Levys will grab any chance we give them and turn it against us. We can't hand them anything." He swept his hand across the table, scattering checkers to the floor. "So, you make another move like that, try to get out of what you've been told, and you'll take an early night. Understand?"

All his force bent toward me. He'd been a fighter pilot before he came home to farm, and I'd never been able to put his bombing missions together with the man who puttered around his house, taught me how to thump a tomato to tell if it was ripe, and made peace. Until now. And he wasn't done. "Now, we've all struggled when this misery came close. Tried all sorts of things."

Surely no one had tried to burn down the Tree before, but I had to make sure. "Like what?"

He shook his head, then bent to pick the checkers up. "You know what." He straightened. "People linking up in a circle, chanting nursery rhymes. Folks cling to all kinds of nonsense when they're terrified." Then his jaw clamped shut.

So, I was right. I was the first to have this plan. And of course I was. Because if someone else had tried to burn down the Tree, we would have all heard that story.

Still, I couldn't leave. Grandad set up one everlasting game after another until darkness took the room, until finally his eyes drooped and his chin sank to his chest. This was my chance. I tiptoed across a maze of creaking boards, grabbed my sneakers, and eased the back door open. And just as I thought I was free, it slipped from my fingers, shut with a bang.

I bolted for the barn in the dusk without looking back, my heart beating so fast it seemed to leap out in front of me. But somehow Grandad slept through all of it, and when I'd gathered what I needed, I took the long way to the woods, hauling along a bucket with a gas can and a shovel.

I pictured him waking with a start, clumping his way to my room and finding me gone with so much at stake. It made me queasy. "Restoration," I muttered to myself. *That's all I'm doing. Jean, awake again.* And when the Burning Tree was gone, destroyed by a Caster, no one could come against any of us anymore. We'd have peace. Real peace. So actually, I was only finishing what Grandad had started.

The dark web of the trees filled the sky. The place the Levys began everything. When we were little, Dad told that story to us most nights, how after the three families had cleared enough land around the Tree to build their houses, Simon Finch logged a disaster in his journal. Only one word. *Fever.* All the Casters made it through, but the Levys and Finches lost children that Simon couldn't bear to name. He scratched seven initials into his records, and then the records stopped. But Jeremiah Levy's anger raged against the Casters for being fortunate, for not losing anyone when he had lost so much, and it turned his mind.

What happened afterward was passed down by word of mouth, and it unwound like a rattler. The Caster children skittered through the August light of the forest, tired and free after being cooped up so long, the purple shooting star they'd picked wilting sweet in their hands. They must have smelled the disaster before they saw it. With no fire lit that day, no lightning strike, no explanation except arson, their house had burned to the ground with their mother and baby sister trapped inside. Next to the ashes, the Tree was scarred but living still, though it was no longer the tree that held up the sky. It was the Burning Tree now.

Benjamin Caster never came home, and that was due to Jeremiah Levy too. He burned the Caster house to the ground, killed the Casters and their baby, and then ran away like the coward he was. And the Tree never forgot. It cursed both our families for its injury, the ones who did the burning and the ones who burned. For generations we'd paid. Jean was paying now. But that would stop tonight.

I was almost at my entrance when I skidded to a stop. Drew sat by the trail, and from the look of the pistachio shell pile next to him, he'd been there a while. When he saw me, he scrambled to his feet, looking taller in the darkness, his blue eyes reflecting the moonlight.

"Hey, Ellie."

"Hi." I tried not to gasp for breath, holding the bucket behind my back.

"I figured I'd catch you here sooner or later." His face held sadness, real sadness, and it made me furious.

"Okay, well, you caught me."

He shifted, ran a hand through his hair. "I was up at the hospital earlier."

"Good for you."

"I thought—you might not want to be alone right now. We could maybe do some sketching or . . ." His voice trailed off.

"It's kind of dark for that."

"Yeah. You turned up later than I figured."

He crossed the space between us like I hadn't been brushing him off since the last time we were in the woods and before I could turn away, he saw the gas can. His face went white.

"Ellie, let's just talk this through, all right?"

He grabbed the handle of the bucket, but I wasn't about to let go. "This isn't . . . what it looks like." But I was too late. He'd already ruined everything. I couldn't go in now, not with a witness, especially one who saw right through me.

"Then I'll walk you home."

"Don't you have a better place to be? You know, on the Levy side of town?"

Drew flinched. "Please don't." He looked down at me in the way that used to send me spinning, but I couldn't give in. Even if he chose me over Charlotte this very second, which wasn't about to happen, Jean was waiting.

"Really, I think that's where you should go," I said. "And don't come back here. I mean it."

His face tightened. "Ellie, are you sure what's happened to

your family—from that mark—just hit Jean? Because you haven't really seemed like yourself. And now, this"—he held up the bucket—"this isn't you."

Rage crashed over me like a breaker. This was who I'd always been. But I couldn't show him that. I couldn't show him anything anymore.

I nodded. "Maybe you're right. I'll go home. I promise."

Drew let go of the bucket, relief flooding his face.

"But I'll be going alone."

"You're making too big a deal of—"

"Goodbye, Drew."

I turned and walked back the way I'd come. A few seconds later, he followed like I knew he would, making sure we both got home safely, me and the gas can. When I disappeared into the brown stalks of Grandad's outlying corn fields, he stood still a moment, a shadow in the darkness, then took off for his house . . . or the sheriff, I didn't know which.

Once he was out of earshot, I ran for the woods like the whole town was after me. The bucket slammed into my knees, the top of the shovel nearly punctured my shoulders, and after that last look on Drew's face, I was running with half of myself missing. Maybe he was right, and the mark had hit me too, taken me apart. But right now, I couldn't think about any of that. Only what I was about to do for my sister.

INSIDE OAKBEND WOODS, I RACED
toward the clearing, my flashlight bouncing off hundreds of
trunks, their branches like feral lace. I had to get to the Burning
Tree before Drew or Grandad or the sheriff found me.

Snapping echoed behind me in the darkness, too high for
footsteps, and I jumped at each pop and crack as if the trees
were after me, like in the community theater play Mom had once
dragged me to where Great-Aunt Ruby was performing. On stage,
she'd become another woman, someone who kept washing and
washing her hands. I believed in the stain she couldn't scrub off.
And in the end, the forest came for her. Now, with the grasping
fingers of those branches at my neck, I wished I'd never seen that
play. With my every step, the trees seemed to change positions.

By the time I made it to the clearing where the Burning Tree
twisted up into the night, I was nothing but fear. The Tree stood
massive in the darkness, shutting out the stars, and the closer
I got, the redder its leaves glinted, which could only mean one
thing. It saw me, knew what I was planning. All around us, the
air throbbed hate like a heartbeat. Still, I ran up to it, grabbed
Jean's squirrel lying limply against its trunk, and backed away.

For Jean, I thought over and over, making myself stay as lines of red crept down the Tree, leaves to branches to trunk.

I dug a firebreak in the dry soil and filled my bucket in the river, but when I poured the water in, the ground steamed, sucked the drops straight down, leaving the surface as dry as ever. There was no time to get upset, no time to think. Drew might be doubling back with the sheriff this very second. I poured bucket after bucket until my arms ached and the clearing around the Tree stayed damp. That would have to be enough.

I dashed some water over my clothes, rubbed it through my hair, and for a second the fresh smell of algae and stone shut out the smoke. After this moment, I wouldn't be Ellie Caster, loner, any longer. I'd be Tree-burner. Protector.

I stepped up to the scarred bulk of the Tree and poured gasoline into all the knotholes I could reach, expecting the branches to fling me away any second. Gasoline splashed down over old Caster initials and, as I made my way to the other side, the Levy ones, though I certainly wasn't doing this for any of them, especially not for Charlotte. This was for Jean. And Grandad. And Sam Caster. All the Casters.

I struck a match and threw it in, then another, and another before I jumped back over the break. The twigs caught first, snagging sparks from bursts of gasoline blaze and flinging fire toward me. Sparks landed in the underbrush just to my right. I ran to them, rolled onto the reaching flames like they'd taught us in school. Some escaped, racing through the tinder of fallen leaves. I pictured Bishop's Gap burning to the ground, lost my mind and tried to put them out with my numb hands, then tore off my jacket and whacked till all the red died out.

I looked up just in time to see the Burning Tree shimmer gold, a giant ember holding heat like a jewel, line after line of initials glowing through its rings. It was almost beautiful. It must have been ripe for the burning because there, right before my eyes, it whitened, then grayed. Then, with a booming sigh, it collapsed.

I stared at the empty clearing until I could really believe the Tree was gone. Bishop's Gap was free. Half a moon smiled down from the sky, the stars had brightened, and I was light enough to float up to them in the clearing air. In a few moments, when I walked into Jean's hospital room, she'd be sitting up, slurping something pink through a straw. And I'd tell her the rhyme, the perfect one I'd thought of for muffin.

I took the fastest way out, the one nearest the hospital, keeping to the shadows by the road. My hands stung, I had burn marks on my jacket, and my shoes were scorched. Grandad would be furious. Dad would ground me till kingdom come. And if the sheriff learned what I'd done, he'd probably lock me up. But it didn't matter. I'd saved my sister.

When I reached the first house on the road, the bob of my flashlight caught something at the bottom of the door, something curved. It looked like the mark, and for a second, my heart stopped, but that was impossible. This was a Finch house. Still, I took the path up to their porch to make sure, tiptoeing past the fake boy holding a fake lantern, and my heart slid down to my ruined shoes.

The mark of the crescent moon looked back at me, its curse on that house. But marks never came again this quickly. And never to the Finches.

I shone my flashlight on the next house, a Levy one this time. That door had the mark too.

So did the third house.

And the fourth.

I froze, choking on charred air. I hadn't ended anything in the woods.

I'd unleashed it.

7

THE STARS THAT SAW EVERYTHING

kept me pinned in place. Everyone would know what I'd done. Drew. My parents. Charlotte Levy. People I'd barely glanced at in the grocery store.

There must be hundreds of houses in Bishop's Gap. And in every single one of them, something catastrophic had just happened, though, for a few moments, I was the only one who knew it. And all because I'd decided to burn a gash right into the center of the woods. *You can't fight fire with fire* pounded through my brain. There was no point in going to the hospital now. Jean wouldn't be better. Then a shredding thought ripped through me. Maybe I'd just made her worse. Maybe she was already gone.

Headlights swung around a distant corner, and my scorched red shoes took me deep into the fields, that stupid shovel banging around in the stupid bucket. I had to get to my sister, make sure she was still breathing, but first I had to dump the evidence.

I couldn't stop shivering, dodging shadow to shadow all the way to Grandad's barn, ignoring the lights at the backs of houses where, maybe, people were discovering what exactly I'd just done to them. When I'd stashed everything in the barn, I tiptoed up to the house for a change of clothes.

I was almost to the door when I saw it—a red emergency light spinning on the oak tree. All the breath left my lungs. Grandad must have found out I was gone and called the sheriff. I wanted to run to the barn and stay there forever, but anyone could see it would be better to stroll in, slow and calm. I arranged my face, practicing what I'd say. "I got a little stir crazy." Grandad always said that, so maybe it would work. And then, "I went out for a walk, just to the fields. I had to. I'm really sorry."

Just in time, I remembered my scorched jacket and rolled it up under my arm. Maybe no one would notice my shoes. I was still practicing, walking toward the lights till they strobed through my whole body, till the words sounded like the truth, when a hand clamped my shoulder, spun me around.

"Ellie."

It was Sheriff Caster, his normally slick-combed hair sticking out in tufts, red flashing across the whites of his eyes.

Before I could say my lines, static burst from his car, "You need to . . . back here. Now." Edna Finch had been dispatching as long as I could remember, but I'd never heard her this frantic. My heart dropped until I remembered this couldn't be about the marks. Not yet.

The sheriff didn't even start toward it, just stared like he'd never seen me before. "Where'd you sneak up from?"

I panicked, forgot the right words. "I was . . . out for a walk."

"Uh-huh."

"Sheriff? *Sheriff*!" Edna was yelling now through the garble for all she was worth. I kept my eyes fixed on the sheriff's, forced myself not to shift them, not to look away.

"Ellie, your Grandad called a while ago. Said there was prowlers or something. You seen anything like that?"

It was me he'd seen, in the field. I shook my head. "No, sir." My voice came out small, completely unconvincing, but he didn't question me further. Instead, his Adam's apple worked up and down, and I realized he looked about as sad as I'd ever seen another human being.

"See, I didn't quite get a chance to ask him. I'm really sorry, Ellie."

I turned in slow motion, like in the movies when it takes half an eternity for the camera to pan to what you can't bear to see but know is coming.

"I was about to take him in. You can ride with us if you like."

I got myself up the steps and through the door branded with the crescent moon.

Grandad sat in his black leather recliner in the middle of the den with its familiar wooden walls. His newspaper had slipped to the floor, and it looked to all the world like he was taking a nap, except for the veins that branched out all over his face. Just like Jean. He must have leaned his head back exactly when the tree gave up the ghost.

Sheriff Caster hoisted Grandad into a fireman's carry. "Get the door, would you?"

I grabbed the bag with my other shoes, pushed the screen door open, and followed Grandad's swinging hand.

Edna was going crazy now. "I'm getting calls . . . all over. Do you copy? Do you . . ." I slid into the rear seat, which reeked of sweat and cider, and the door shut on her voice.

In the silence, I removed my sneakers and stashed them in my bag, trying not to look at the sheriff buckling Grandad into the passenger seat, the nightmare of what I'd done to him. We flashed through streets so fast I couldn't see the mark on any of the doors, but a block from the hospital I knew what they'd done. Two lines of honking cars snaked from the ER entrance all the way around the block. People ran from their cars with babies or toddlers cradled in their arms. Others staggered forward under the weight of a mother or brother. My fine arts teacher, Adele Levy, tugged someone from the passenger seat of her Buick, tears streaming down her face.

The sheriff switched his siren on, and the car jerked forward, pulling through side streets around to the crowded south entrance. He screeched to the curb and Grandad's head slumped forward. I unbuckled, but before I could even rap on the window, the sheriff had Grandad out of the car and was running with him like he wasn't a dead weight.

I pulled on the door handle that couldn't open, then banged on the window till I'd bruised my hands. I screamed, but no one heard me in the chaos of panicked people rushing past the car, lights flashing on veined faces.

When the world fell silent, I slumped in the seat, shaking at what I'd just done to Bishop's Gap.

8

THE MINUTE HAND ON THE
dashboard clicked up and up and up, and still the sheriff didn't
come. Before I could stop myself, I was sobbing, the wrench of
each breath shudderingly deep until the door screeched open,
letting in ashy air.

"Room 51," Sheriff Caster said. "Sorry it took me so long to
get back. It's a madhouse in—"

I didn't hear the rest. I darted out and flew the hundred steps
to where Jean was. Madhouse didn't begin to describe it. Past the
gliding doors, people slumped everywhere, Levys and Casters
jumbled together, filling the halls with perfume and woodsmoke
and baby powder, like the hospital had just swallowed the town.
The crowd broke only for nurses hurrying through with rolling
beds, so I jumped behind one and stayed with it, scanning the
faces in all the open-doored rooms. I couldn't remember which
room Jean was in, couldn't focus my thoughts with the paging of
doctors and the steady beat over the PA system: *external triage,
external triage, external . . .*

Jean's name came clear against the blur. I fell out of the
current and ran to my sister's room. Mom sat beside her, holding
her hand. From the look on her face, I thought Jean was gone.

But the veins on my sister's face hadn't changed, and her machine still beat jagged lines forward.

Mom looked up when I came in.

"Is she—she's not worse, is she?"

Dad stepped out from the corner of the room. "She's holding steady." His glance fell to my bag. "I thought I told you to stay at Grandad's."

"But Grandad—he's—they had to bring him in too." On the other side of the door, muffled steps kept pounding by.

Dad looked shocked. "His heart?"

"No. He's like Jean. Lots of . . ." I choked on the words before I managed to get them out. "Lots of people are."

Dad stared at me a moment, then sank into a chair. "It can't be."

Mom came to me, searching my face. "But you're okay? Please tell me you're okay." When I nodded, she turned to Dad. "Jamie, how could this happen?"

"No idea." His voice sounded like someone had punched the words out of him. He glanced at my shoes, but this pair didn't give me away. Still, I wanted to tell him, yell that this was all my fault just so I could hear them say it would be all right. But that was impossible now. No one could pretend the world back to normal, not anymore.

In the silence, I walked to the other side of Jean's bed and took her hand. The shock of its pulse jolted up my arm. "Jean," I whispered, "you can come back now. Please. I've thought of the right word."

"What was that?" Mom asked.

"Nothing. Just about one of her poems." And then, before either of them could ask me anything else, I added, "I should find Grandad. Make sure he's comfortable. The sheriff said Room 51."

"Sheriff Caster?" Dad straightened like some unseen puppeteer had pulled all his strings taut. I shouldn't have mentioned that. "I'm coming with you," he said, tucking in his shirt. His tone grew stern. "And then, Ellie, you're going to tell us everything."

After Dad took me to look in on Grandad, lying helpless under crisp hospital corners, I tried to explain why the sheriff had come to Grandad's house. I told them about the imaginary prowler, went over the lie so many times that by midnight my words had gone stale and Jean's room was a high-pressure system. On the other side of the door, the hospital finally quieted somewhat, but footsteps still echoed down the hall and beds squeaked past all night, constant reminders of what I'd done pressing down on me till I could hardly breathe. I'd released something beyond imagining, though that didn't make sense. The Tree caused the marks—tonight had proved that. So now that it was gone, why weren't the marks gone too?

As the gray dawn slipped under the blinds, lighting up the pattern of veins on my sister's face, the one that looked like roots branching out, I sat up so abruptly that, for a fraction of a second, Mom took her eyes off Jean.

I had to get to the library. Maybe it would hold the answer, something about trees I'd overlooked, their root systems maybe. And anywhere would be better than here. Before I could think up some excuse, the bright lights of the fake hospital morning switched on and Dad stood up, his face worn. "What can I get you for breakfast, Arden?"

"Coffee."

"And?"

"Just coffee."

"You really ought to—"

"Please don't talk 'ought' me, Jamie." Her voice held an edge I'd rarely heard.

"Fine. Just coffee. Ellie, you're coming with me."

I launched from the chair, ignoring the ache of my bruises from last night. The hospital cafeteria was one step closer to outside, though the walk down the crowded halls lasted an eternity. People had sorted themselves out by now, Levys on one side, Casters on the other, Finches and everyone else scattered in between. At the cafeteria, Dad stuck a tray in my hands and headed for the coffee. Every few seconds, he glanced back, so I'd have to wait until he was distracted at the cash register to escape. I plodded along with a line of messy-haired, stricken-looking people, trying not to think about how I'd taken someone from every single person here.

I'd just spooned a token plop of oatmeal into my bowl when a few feet ahead, tongs clanked against metal. Adelina Levy swung around, yelling, "You idiot!" She was in my class, one of Charlotte's satellites, and she had her finger in Steven Caster's face. "You just got bacon smut on the grapefruit. I can't eat anything here now."

"Oh, that's a real tragedy," Steven said, grabbing the tongs and slamming them into the bacon. "You'll have to wipe it off." Any other day it would have ended there. But now all the Levys in line pressed forward. They circled Steven, and the rest of us froze as the grief in the room tilted into anger, just like that. I wanted to jump in, stop them, but that would just shove everyone over the edge.

"Sorry," Steven muttered, breaking through the circle and taking off down one of the corridors. All over the cafeteria, Casters stepped out to block anyone who might try to follow him, but no one did. The truce held. For now.

As the room took a breath, someone grabbed my elbow. I turned, my body tensing, but it wasn't a Levy who had hold of my arm. It was Drew. Without his usual smile, his face looked older, more chiseled. Even now, at the end of everything, he turned my knees weak.

Drew pointed to the trash cans in the corner. "We have to talk. Now."

"I can't. I'm on my way to—my mom hasn't had breakfast."

"Now, Ellie."

He turned, and I followed him. He'd seen me with a gas can, and he knew what had happened next. If there was any chance of finishing what I'd started, I needed to keep him from telling anyone.

"Well, look who it is." Curtis Finch, Drew's cousin, stood by the stalls of cereal, setting a third bowl of Lucky Charms on a tray already piled high with bacon as we walked by. "Andrew and his girlfriend." Curtis smirked at me, running a hand through greasy red hair, his pond-water eyes glinting. "No wait, you're the not-girlfriend, aren't you? You're just the one he spends every waking minute with."

Drew's shoulders stiffened. And Dad was watching from the other side of the cafeteria, which made everything worse.

"Not the time," Drew said without breaking his stride. As

soon as we stepped behind the trash cans, he faced me, ashen. "Ellie, what did you do?"

"Nothing. I went home. You saw me."

"Come on, you can't carry this alone. I know you didn't mean for this to happen. Just tell them. It will be okay. I'll go with you, and then they can . . ."

Even last night hadn't pushed him away, and for a second, I wanted to pretend he was right, do exactly what he said. But that wouldn't get him back from Charlotte. And it wouldn't help Jean.

"Tell who? And they'll do what, exactly?" I stepped away from him. "It wasn't me, Drew. I was thinking about, you know, but I didn't do it."

He narrowed his eyes. "You're saying it's just coincidence that you walk up to the woods with what you were carrying and then half the town goes down?"

The tile pattern of the wall—three white squares and two green diamonds—swam behind him, and I almost threw up right there between the trash and the scrambled eggs, hearing it from him.

"Come on," he urged. "We tell each other, that's the pact. Remember?"

"Someone else must have gotten there first." I'd never lied like this to him before, never lied like this to anyone. "It's not what you think. Please, Drew."

He didn't say anything for so long I started to worry.

"Look, you're not going to tell anyone, right? They won't believe I didn't do it."

"You think I'd tell people I saw what you were planning and didn't stop you?" Drew's eyes gleamed dark. "You've made me part of this, too. You have to tell them, Ellie. They'll find out soon enough, anyway."

"I think I can fix it," I whispered. "I just need a little more time."

"Ellie," he said, putting his hands on my shoulders, his touch electric. "You can't stop this. And I know you. This secret will eat you alive."

"I just need a little more time," I repeated, the only thing I could think to say.

His hands slipped to his side, disappointment twisting his face, then anger. "I have to go." He turned away from me without another glance, walked through the cafeteria, and disappeared down an antiseptic hall.

9

I BLINKED AWAY THE TEARS
stinging my eyes. Drew had made his choice and I'd made mine, and there was no time to wallow in any of it. Dad was nowhere in sight, so there was a clear shot to the exit.

"Ellie," I heard him call from a far table as I bolted through the door into an overcast morning. But I didn't turn around, not till I was sure I'd outpaced him.

At the library, the door was locked, which didn't matter. Miss Prow had opened early for me before. It wasn't until I'd rattled the knob and knocked on the glass, watching for her to come out of the staff room, that I remembered. She was the only librarian, and she lived alone, so no one could open this place. The mark on her door had seen to that.

I thought of how she'd run bent fingers down a line of books, stopping at a shabby cover with the binding nearly rubbed off. "Yes," she'd say. "This is the right one for you." When I turned back to Main Street, it was out of focus, blurred by tears.

Most of the stores were closed. A harsh breeze whipped the awnings over Meet and Three's dark windows, and half the lights were out at County Grocers, like they stood for the people who weren't there. For Grandad, who'd been flipping the pages of his paper in a circle of lamplight, waiting for me to come back. For Jean, crying herself to sleep because of what I'd said. For all the people I'd just silenced.

But the hush of this town wouldn't last long. As soon as the shock wore off, Bishop's Gap would tear itself apart. From what I'd seen down at the cafeteria, that might not even take a day. And I couldn't stop any of it.

A spit of rain splattered the sidewalk, and the town went gray, except for one block down, where, from a store that had been closed as long as I could remember, fresh yellow light spilled out onto the sidewalk.

———

By the time I reached the lighted window, I was drenched from the downpour, but I couldn't make myself go in. This was the old five and dime, the place everyone whispered was haunted. On the door, ornate black letters spelled out something new.

Blooms.
Coffee, Tea & What-You-Will.

Through the rain-streaked window, white tables floated like islands on a blue tile floor. All empty, of course. Whoever owned this place had picked the worst possible time to open again, but it didn't look like there'd be ghosts. It seemed warm. Safe, even. *They're not from around here,* Dad had said, and right now, I'd take anything that wasn't part of this town. I'd go in and dry off, just for a minute, if only to pull my thoughts together. And really, there was nowhere else to go.

I pushed the door open to another world, a room heavy with roasted beans and chocolate and the faintest hint of licorice, like the scratch-and-sniff stickers in Jean's book. It wrapped itself around me, a bright circle of caffeinated calm, and I was just thawing around the edges when I saw the last person I could handle with half the town dying. Charlotte Levy sat at the white counter up front, her hair shining gold under the hanging lamps, the fear on her face dissolving into the expression that always slammed me up against the wall.

Of all the people to survive the mark on her door.

In that instant, I knew I had forest mulch hanging off my pants and about a thousand pulls in my sweater, and I knew why Drew couldn't keep his eyes off her, not that any of it mattered now.

I was turning to head back out when a woman I'd never seen before stepped out from behind Charlotte. In the rain-washed light, the woman's brown hair and blue dress seemed to shimmer, phantom-like. She was clearly not from anywhere around Bishop's Gap, though she didn't have that just-passing-through look about her, either.

"Order's up, Ellie."

That stopped me in my tracks, and it wasn't just because she knew my name. It was her voice. Not ghostly, but wild, like water from the center of the earth.

"I–I didn't order anything."

"Just come up here, please, and check that it's right."

As rain dashed against the windows, I walked past the white tables, every step echoing on the floor, ignoring Charlotte's narrowed eyes. Clearly, coming in here had been a mistake.

"Yours." The woman set a plate in front of me. "And yours." A second plate clanked down in front of Charlotte.

Mine held a bowl of okra drowned in ketchup, like Dad's after he carved Jean's initials into the Burning Tree. Next to it sat a muffin, iced like a pink button.

"What rhymes with muffin, Ellie?" Jean had asked.

Button. The word I hadn't told anyone.

I froze. This had to be a joke, another trick, and I steeled myself for the smirk that was sure to be on Charlotte's face, but she was staring down at her own plate. Toast layered with peanut butter and circles of banana, drizzled with chocolate syrup and sprinkles.

The woman's face gave nothing away.

"This isn't what I ordered," Charlotte said, slipping a few strands of hair behind her ear and showing the scar on her forehead, something she only did when she was nervous. "I just want coffee."

The woman set a full mug down by the toast without a hint of expression in her clear brown eyes. I'd never seen a face so unwrinkled. Not a worry line, not a hint of past smiles at her mouth. Who was this person who'd just appeared like magic in our town? Even Jean had creases from scrunching up her face while she drew her endless unicorns.

Charlotte pushed at the mug. "This was supposed to be to go."

"Not yet. We're still waiting for the other one."

"What are you talking about?"

"The other member of your party."

"We're not a party," Charlotte and I said at the same time, and Charlotte slid her plate further from mine. "I'm not with her."

The woman turned her back to us and poured another mug

of coffee from a steaming pot. "The door's open if you want to leave."

Rain lashed the street outside, and neither of us moved. I couldn't, not with that muffin pinning me there like an anchor.

"If I'm going to stay," Charlotte declared, "I want to know what's going on."

The woman was stirring coffee in a huge stone mug, her eyes vague like she'd forgotten we were standing there. Finally, they flickered over us. "This is a conversation. Or at least it will be soon."

I couldn't manage a word with my pulse hammering out to my fingertips. We were being drawn into something, maybe a web, maybe a current. Whatever it was, I didn't want to be anywhere near it with Charlotte.

"And what exactly is this?" Charlotte pointed a manicured nail at her extravagant toast.

"That's proof."

"Of what?"

"What I'm about to tell you."

"In the conversation." Charlotte rolled her eyes.

"Yes."

Then I understood. Somehow, this woman knew what I'd done, just like she knew about the okra and the muffin. She was going to tell everything, but before I had a chance to take off for the city limits and then keep going, the door jangled. I didn't even look around. It was Drew, had to be. He and Charlotte together would witness the disclosing of what I'd done and make this particular nightmare complete.

"Well, looky here," said the last member of our party.

It wasn't Drew.

10

THE WOMAN MADE US SIT together at one of the little island tables and then took a seat herself, simply staring into space, her face calm and wild. Charlotte pushed her toast around her plate with a fork, while Drew's cousin Curtis hammered down on a plateful of mini quiche like he hadn't just eaten half the hospital breakfast buffet, leering at Charlotte like she was a double malt. Which only made sense. As long as I could remember, he'd been under her spell.

I clasped my hands in my lap so no one could see them shake while I waited for this woman to tell them everything. I couldn't run away, couldn't leave Jean. And I couldn't hide my mistake forever. So, this was as good a time as any for them to find out what I'd done to the town.

Curtis finally came up for air, though he didn't take his eyes off Charlotte. "Hey, I never thought I'd see Levy and Caster at the same table," he said. "Especially the two of you. Not without a little face-scratching, am I right?" He clawed the air and made some kind of meowing sound with his mouth full.

"Gag me," said Charlotte.

"Can you believe it out there? I stopped at County's for some jerky and chips and stuff. Just about all that's left on their shelves are batteries and cream soda. Thought I was gonna starve or something."

Get it over with, I thought, staring at the woman's blank face. *Please.*

Curtis lifted his mug in the woman's direction. "You're a lifesaver. I didn't catch your name?"

It seemed to take her a moment to remember we were there. "Maggie," she said.

"Maggie Caster? Levy? Finch?"

"Just Maggie."

Something about her tone made even Curtis go quiet. When he'd scarfed down the rest of the quiche, he pushed his chair back from the table, wiping the corners of his cold-sore mouth. "I didn't bring my wallet. Can one of you spot me?"

"Just a moment, Mr. Finch," Maggie stopped him. "You are here this morning, each of you, because I have an opportunity to offer."

I had been so sure she was about to turn on me, I couldn't quite comprehend what she'd just said.

"I will make this offer to you together, as a group."

"It's a free hotel room, isn't it?" said Curtis, grinning. "In the Bermudas. And all we have to do is sell our souls or something."

"Shut up, Curtis," said Charlotte. Under her foundation, she'd blanched.

"In two hours, the CDC will arrive. In two hours and fifteen minutes, your town will be under quarantine. And Oakbend Woods, of course."

"That's kind of creepy," said Curtis. "Kind of specific."

"Shut. Up." Charlotte stabbed her fork in his direction.

"Okay, okay." Curtis lifted his hands. "I'm just saying. It's been a weird day."

"The CDC will not be able to help, but of course you already know that," Maggie went on as if no one had spoken. Now she was talking right to me. "There's only one reversal possible. You need to move the Oakbend River, the three of you. And *only* the three of you."

Charlotte startled as I pushed away from the table. I wasn't about to go back into the woods—or anywhere else—with these two.

"Wha-a-at?" Curtis laughed awkwardly. "That's ridiculous. I don't—what does that even mean?"

"Just what I said. The river in the woods was moved from its original course. That was not meant to be. Your task is to move it back."

"That's crazy," Charlotte stated, and for once she was right. I hated agreeing with a Levy, but the three of us trying to move the Oakbend River, even if it was more of a creek in places, that was insane.

"I'm sorry," I said, nudging my chair farther back for a straight path to the door, "but the Oakbend? That doesn't—I mean, that can't have anything to do with . . . what's happening at the hospital."

"Can't it?" Maggie said, her fingernails tinking a faint rhythm on her mug. She didn't look crazy. If anything, she looked larger than life, saner than the rest of us. "Well, you won't know that until you try, will you? But if you do nothing—" The tinking stopped. "If you do nothing, without a question, they will die."

I could already see that for myself. *Reversal* echoed in my mind, a glimmer of hope for Grandad and Jean and Miss Prow.

I pulled my chair back in.

A flicker of a smile crossed Maggie's lips, then vanished like it had never been. "I know how it sounds. And Charlotte, I know it's not your birthday." She pointed to the bananas piled on top of Charlotte's toast. "But still, a circle for each year."

"How did you—" began Charlotte, her eyes suddenly too big for her face.

"Ellie," Maggie said, turning to me, "you found the rhyme." She nodded at the muffin. "And the world is crammed full of sadness, yes." The exact words I'd thought after my conversation with Dad. "But joy too—and mystery."

Tears pricked my eyes, here in front of everyone. If I let them fall now, I'd never stop, and Maggie must have known that because she said smoothly, "Would you like another quiche, Curtis?" And then no one was looking at me anymore. Curtis had put his hand around his empty plate like he was trying to protect it. "Those were the best he could do," Maggie said. "He emptied his pockets, cleaned out the whole freezer section."

"Yeah," Curtis muttered. "And then he left." It was easy enough to figure out the rest. I pictured Curtis alone in a dark kitchen, heating up frozen mini quiche while he waited for his father who wasn't coming back.

"Need I go on?" she said.

When we all just stared blankly at her, she put down the mug. "Ellie, your grandmother wrote poems like Jean. She kept them in a shoebox under her front porch." That would be at Grandad's house. My grandmother had grown up there, and I didn't go out and check. I already believed her, and anyway, there was no time.

"Your scar, Charlotte . . ."

"Stop," Charlotte hissed.

"Your scar came from the marble-top table."

Charlotte shrank into herself.

"And Curtis." He looked up tentatively like she was about to hit him. "The bird your grandfather whittled, it isn't lost. You'll find it behind your dresser."

"So, what, you've been spying on us?" demanded Charlotte, though her voice came out thin. She knew as well as I did that spying wouldn't give Maggie all she'd told us. The woman would have to have been here for more than one lifetime. A chill skittered down my spine. Maybe the stories were right. This place had been haunted all along, and Maggie was the ghost. Though she seemed too solid for that. Too substantial. But we were in Bishop's Gap, after all. Anything could happen here.

"I remember from before the marks began," Maggie told us, and in a trick of the light she seemed to shimmer. "So, trust me when I tell you that you need to move the river."

The room fell silent. I'd never seen Curtis quiet for so long. But we couldn't just sit here in a daze while the town went on dying. "And if we do that, you're saying we'll fix things. Everyone will all be okay."

"Perhaps," she remarked. "That will be up to you."

I wanted to ask Maggie lots of other things too, since apparently, she knew how the curse worked, how the Tree put marks on our doors, how it had tricked me. But even if there was time for answers, she'd already stood up, collecting our plates.

"You've been looking in the wrong section, Ellie," she said, stacking our full plates on top of Curtis's empty one. Then she stopped and looked me right in the eye. I could barely breathe, like she'd plunged me underwater. "Not botany. Myths."

"Whatever that means," Charlotte muttered. But as soon as Maggie disappeared into the kitchen, she found her full voice again. "Hey," she called. "Why us?"

At first there was only silence, as if Maggie had evaporated into nothing on the other side of the wall. Then her voice floated out, clear and distant. "Because you walked through my door."

For a second, we stared at each other. Then Charlotte rose so fast the table swayed. "Well, I'm out."

She was going to leave all those people stranded in some neverland. Jean, Grandad, her own family. Everyone I'd hurt. Fear wrenched my stomach as I jumped up, too, and blocked her exit. "Look, you don't get to choose for us."

She stepped around me, gripping her purse—some plaid name-brand thing she carried so she wouldn't look like she was from around here—and stalked toward the café door as if I hadn't said a word. Just like a Levy.

I wanted to turn my back and pretend I didn't care until I made it true. But this time I couldn't go hide in the forest. This time there was way too much at stake.

I ran after her with Curtis behind me into the last chilly gasp of the raindrops.

"Like I said," she yelled over her shoulder, "this is crazy. So, you can stop right there."

"That woman knows things," I called after her. "Impossible things. So maybe she knows how to make everyone well."

Charlotte spun around. "Or she's a leech. Feeds on the gullibles." She pulled out a matching plaid umbrella and stabbed it at the sky. She had that look on her face, like she ruled the planets. "The woods are forbidden for a reason. And I'm not going anywhere with a Caster. Especially you." Then she turned on Curtis. "I'm certainly not going with the idiot."

"Hey," he protested and then winked, "I'd move oceans for *you*."

She rolled her eyes, but she hadn't actually left, not yet, so it was time to beg. "Look, it doesn't matter what you think of me,"

I said to her. "We have to try. Please. Even if it's a billion-to-one chance it works."

"You've got the odds right, anyway," she snapped.

Curtis stepped up beside me. "Look, Ellie has a point. This is obviously off the rails, but what do we lose trying?"

I hadn't expected that. Then again, I hadn't spent more than about thirty seconds at a time with him for years. Curtis Finch used to be the little red-haired kid running around town with a slingshot and a squirt gun. Now he haunted the underbelly of Bishop's Gap.

"And it's not like there's anything else to do," he said, gesturing at all the closed stores.

"Maybe not for you." She turned on her heel.

I said the only thing I had left to stop her. "What was the toast about, Charlotte?" She flinched, the umbrella trembling above her head. I lowered my voice. "Who are you losing down at the hospital?"

"That is none of your business."

I shivered in my soaked pullover, watching my sister's last chance slip through my fingers, kicking myself for being surprised. This was Charlotte, after all. I only wished Drew was here to see her walk away.

Then it hit me. This was Charlotte, which meant I'd been trying all the wrong words. She specialized in threats. "You know, do what you want," I called after her. "I don't care. I'm going into the woods and if it breaks everything, it breaks everything."

She spun around. "You wouldn't." Then she stopped, and I held my breath. Raindrops tapped at my shoulder while the town hung in the balance.

Finally, her shoulders sagged. "No, you absolutely would. So, someone has to go with you, don't they? Make sure you don't mess up and wipe the rest of us out."

My heart didn't have time to soar because she walked back toward us slowly, one foot in front of the other, balance-beam style, keeping her eyes on me like a snake. When she got close enough, her words hissed out too. "But when you're wrong, you'll wish this day had never happened, you and that Maggie person both."

I ignored her, which was probably going to be the key to surviving this.

"You're in, right, Curtis?" I asked Drew's cousin.

He grinned, though a shadow hung behind his eyes. "You know it. I wouldn't miss this show."

"This is crazy," Charlotte said again, like she was stuck on that one word.

But it wasn't. It was perfect. We'd head into the woods, Charlotte would complain that her heels were sinking into the mud the whole time, and Curtis would do exactly what he always did with group projects, which was nothing. But we'd be together like Maggie wanted. And once they gave up, which couldn't take long, I'd fix the mess I'd made, alone and unaided. Then everything would be set right. No more Burning Tree. No more curse.

Right on cue, a watery sun broke through the clouds.

"What the heck does it mean to put the river back?" asked Curtis.

I shrugged. The less I helped these two, the better.

Charlotte sighed. "It means, idiot, we're going into Oakbend Woods."

11

THE BACK ROADS TO THE WOODS

were empty, but the stench of burning rubber still hung in the air from everyone's race to the hospital the night before. I tried to shut those pictures out, swallow the bitter taste that rose in my mouth, but the closer we got, the darker the trees loomed, as if the storm clouds clearing from the sky had all gathered there.

Curtis didn't seem to notice, the usual stale grin plastered on his face. "So, what do you think'll happen when we, you know, do the thing?" He pushed his red hair back from his forehead. "The earth splits, that weird Tree falls in, and everybody gets saved?"

"Nothing," Charlotte replied curtly. She stalked along, eyes forward, like we were her personal inconvenience. Her unnecessary plaid umbrella skittered patterns across her face. "That's what happens. Not one thing."

She'd made it clear she was only coming to control the damage, but she was wrong. Once I moved the river, we'd see something beautiful for once—the remedy. Though I couldn't quite imagine how.

When we reached the parking lot by the mouth of the woods, Charlotte finally snapped her umbrella closed. "Fantastic," she said, knocking gravel from her heels. "We've arrived." She'd been here for the Levy ceremony just two months before, but you'd never know it from her poise. And that was all Drew saw when he looked at her. Perfection. I pulled a loose string from my drenched pullover, wishing anyone else had walked into Maggie's café.

"Let's get this over with." I led the way to the entrance. It was the last place I wanted to be with a Levy and a wild card, but the sooner we started, the sooner we'd be done.

One step in, the woods fought back. Even after the rain, clouds of ash swirled up to the dying leaves, stinging my eyes. I breathed splinters. This was the Burning Tree screaming what I'd done, exposing me, and I halted. How could I find anything in here? How could anyone?

"This is some messed-up snow." Curtis's eyes watered, and he'd finally stopped smiling.

Charlotte surprised me by grabbing my arm as she coughed. "I want to see exactly what's happened." She pulled me down the path, heading straight for the Burning Tree, but I couldn't face that place, not yet. And certainly not with her.

"We don't have time," I rasped, jerking away. "We need to find the spot where the river leaves the woods, follow its course up from there."

"The river flows by the Tree. That's where we'll find it."

"But if we head the wrong direction, we'll have to double back," I said. "We'll waste all that time." I'd have to tip my hand, just a little. "Look, I've been in here. Once, a long time ago. I know a shortcut."

Charlotte wavered, loosening her grip on my sleeve, and I held my breath. Then she nodded. "Show us."

The fastest way would be left, skirting the patch of poison ivy by the birches, following my old footpaths. In a quarter mile, we'd reach the river. But those paths would give away how often I'd come to this place. I couldn't afford a Levy knowing that, so I led them straight into the underbrush where the holly was thickest.

Behind me, I heard Charlotte say, "You first, idiot."

"Hey. Quit calling me that." The edge in Curtis's voice made me spin around, but he was grinning, gazing down at Charlotte again like she was dessert.

"So, give me a reason not to." She waved us on. "I'm keeping my eyes on the both of you."

For a second, I could have throttled her for treating us like Levy property. But that wouldn't help my sister. When we finally got moving, Curtis crashed through the underbrush with his steel-toed boots, leaving a path even the deputies of Bishop's Gap could follow.

We were in far enough that every breath seared when he spoke. "So, I've been thinking," he said, "when we get to the river, we'll have to figure out how deep it is. Then we'll know what kind of structure to build."

It wasn't a terrible idea. Maybe Curtis wouldn't be a deadweight after all.

Charlotte's footsteps stopped and we turned. "Structure?" She swatted at a twig with her purse. "I hope you're not expecting me to actually touch any of this."

"No, Charlotte," I said, "no one's expecting anything of you."

Before she could bite back, I bent to inspect a strand of kudzu like it could tell me where the old riverbed was. But all I saw was the ash strangling everything, drowning all the plants that weren't already dormant, while the veined faces of everyone I'd hurt seemed to press in around me. I could almost hear their whispered *hurry*.

"You're lost, aren't you?" said Charlotte, glaring down at me. "This is the one thing you ought to be able to do, forest freak."

Forest freak. The world reeled as I stood to face her. Somehow, she knew I'd come in here more than once. And then it hit me. Drew had told her, which meant even when he was with her, he still thought about me. She crossed her arms, and I understood something else now too. Against all odds, Charlotte Levy was jealous—of me. For a second, I couldn't help a faint glimmer of hope, but I shut it down just as fast. I couldn't risk distraction. And none of that changed who Drew had chosen.

Curtis held up a hand. "Hey, give her a second, princess. She just said it's been a long time since she was here."

"That's right," I said, trying to keep up the act, "I'm pretty sure the river's this way."

Distraction or not, I would have given anything for Drew to be here with me. At some point, he'd have to glance away from Charlotte. "Steady," he'd say. "Steady. You'll find it. You know this place better than anyone." Then he'd put an arm around me, pull me close till there was nothing between us but electricity. And then he'd bend down—

Stop it, Ellie.

We could hear the river now, swollen with rainwater, gushing around the bend and out to freedom.

———

"I could have found this faster myself," Charlotte complained as we stood on the bank, watching the water leave the broken woods. I'd never expected either of them to make it this far. And it was just light enough here to see she had a scratch across her cheekbone. Of course, like in the movies.

Curtis had picked up a stick somewhere and now he was twirling it between his fingers. "So, before we launch this building project, should we try a little Maggie magic?"

Charlotte shot him a look. "You *have* to be kidding."

I shrugged. "You know what? Go for it. It wouldn't be stranger than anything else in Bishop's Gap."

"You got that right." Curtis waved the stick at the river like he was conducting it. For a second, I almost expected some ray of light to point the way. But nothing happened, and he turned back around, surveying the decomposing branches on the forest floor. "So, magic was a bust."

"Well, this isn't the right place anyway," I said, before he wasted any time trying to move the river here. "We need to find the old bed." My words came out like it would be that simple. But no matter how clearly I pictured every square inch of the woods, I still couldn't come up with anything like Maggie described. I'd need time alone to unearth it. "We should divide up," I suggested. "Curtis, you and Charlotte take the other bank. I'll search for the old bed on this side."

Curtis's eyes sparked. "Deal."

"No way," said Charlotte. "I'm not going anywhere alone with you, idiot. Got that? Ever. You take that other bank. I'm going with Ellie."

I took a muddy step back. "Not a chance." I couldn't look for clues to an old riverbed with her shimmering along next to me.

It hadn't seemed possible, but her glares were getting icier. "I meant what I said before. Someone has to keep a Caster from destroying what's left of Bishop's Gap. You weren't supposed to come in here, but you did. And now you've sucked the rest of us in too."

She took off down the squelchy bank, stilettoing her way past the three aspens, the ones bent together like sisters talking with their arms around each other. I used to sketch those trees over and over. Now they'd turned their backs to me.

"Yell when you find something," Curtis called after her. He kept his tone light as usual, but around his cold sores, his face had gone splotchy. She'd finally sliced through his armor. And I'd lost too, which was worst case scenario because the river would lead Charlotte straight to the last place I wanted to be alone with her—the center of the woods where the Burning Tree had stood.

I'd just have to find the old bed before we reached it.

12

BUT OF COURSE, NOTHING
showed itself, no grooves or sediment or anything else that
indicated an old riverbed, almost like the woods were hiding it,
driving us further in. With each step, my breath stabbed deeper
until nothing but dread raced through my veins. Charlotte
already knew I'd spent time in the woods with Drew. If she
figured out what I'd done, I'd never move the river. The Levys
would come for us, and I'd be dead before the sun set. My whole
family would. Maybe every Caster.

When we finally reached the clearing where I'd burned the
Tree, I couldn't breathe at all. The stench of wet rot turned my
stomach, nearly doubling me over. Next to me, Charlotte clapped
her hand over her mouth and, for once, I understood exactly how
she felt.

Ash filled the empty space as if the ghosts of everyone the
curse had touched hung there, suspended in the air. The river
cut through the ground like a scar.

I'd never imagined anything I could do would look like this.

Back at the café, Maggie had said *myth*, and now, standing
in this nightmare emptiness, worse than when the Tree had
been there, I knew what she meant. Whatever I'd unleashed was

bigger than Levy and Caster. Bigger even than Bishop's Gap. So, I had to find the old bed, and I had to find it fast. If not, Jean's sickness would just be the beginning.

Charlotte hadn't moved, her hand frozen at her mouth, but guilt had to be written all over my face.

"We should go," I tried to whisper, but the ash filled my throat, cutting off my words. Before I could try again, Curtis stepped out from the fog on the other side of the river, the flame of his red hair barely visible under the coat of white ash. Apparently, he'd been keeping pace with us. "Well, here you are, princess," he said. Then his eyes darted to me, clouded, unsteady. Nothing was stable here.

I swallowed down the cinders. "Can you believe it's gone?" I spun out the only explanation I could come up with. "Must have been lightning."

"Yeah, it smells like a lightning strike," Curtis said, snapping a smile back on. "Really strong." He pulled a bottle from his pocket and spritzed it all over himself until even at that distance he reeked of eucalyptus.

Charlotte wrinkled her nose. "That is a *room freshener,*" she said disdainfully. She turned to me, slipping strands of hair behind her ear, forgetting to pull them back over her scar. "And what it smells like here is gasoline."

"Cool," Curtis said, pumping in every direction.

She whirled on him. "This isn't stand-up, Curtis. Not everything's a joke."

Curtis pocketed the bottle, his jaw clenched. "Hey, I got family sick too. But you have to do something to get through it, am I right?"

"Yes," I said through the catch in my throat. "And there's nothing here that looks like the old bed. We should move on."

"That's all you have to say to this?" Charlotte's voice shook, the scar on her forehead whitening. "The Tree's gone and that's all you have to say? You're such a Caster." Behind her, the ashes seemed to glow, embers everywhere, and for a second, I itched to drag her out of my forest, let the whole town burn if it had to.

But if I lashed out, that would make me just like her. I let out a breath, forcing myself to think of my sister till the embers died. "There's nothing we can do for anyone here. So let's just finish and get out."

Charlotte leaned forward. "Ellie, if this doesn't work—and believe me, it's not going to—I'm telling everyone you come in here." She waved her hand toward the clearing. "I get it. You understand that? And they'll know too."

An image of the Levys coming for my family flashed across my mind, but I didn't give her the satisfaction of reacting. "We're moving on," I called to Curtis.

"Just like that? No last words for the magic tree?" When neither of us answered, he mock-saluted. "Roger that. Moving on."

On the other side of the clearing, Charlotte took one step into a tangle of vines and wobbled, lurched, and threw her arms up for balance. Before I could stop her, she fell into a puddle of mud where the ground sloped down from the creek bank.

"Are you hurt?" I asked, picking my way over to her, trying to keep the hope from my voice. Beyond her, soggy leaves filled a long groove that deepened as I traced my foot along it. My pulse hammered. This had to be it, the old riverbed. I'd never noticed it here before, blind to everything but the Burning Tree. Now I was so close to helping Jean I could taste it, sweet against the ash.

Charlotte sat up, brushing muddy leaves from her shirt. One clung to her hair, stuck out like a feather. "I'm fine," she said tersely. "Except for this." She held out a broken-off, mud-coated heel. The woods had finally done their work, and the triumph of that must have shown on my face because in a sudden motion she snatched both shoes off and flung them into the trees, where they swung like strange ornaments.

A branch thudded down next to us and Curtis hopped from it. "I heard some kind of crash. Did you fall off your pedestal or some—" His voice broke as he poked a foot into the leaves, then paced a few steps down, kicking the sides of the hidden trench. "Well, look what you stumbled into, princess! Just what we came in here for." He squinted back at the creek. "And the river's not too deep here. I'd say, what, four feet at the most?"

So much for outlasting them.

Curtis glanced around. "Okay, we need to build some kind of aqueduct, force the water that direction."

"A dam would be faster," I said.

Curtis's eyebrows lifted, then he gave an energetic thumbs up. "That could work—there's plenty of sticks lying around. We can have this done by dinner." He leaned toward Charlotte. "Then we'll go down to Meet and Three's, have us some chicken-fried everything, won't we, sweetheart?"

She rolled her eyes and he flashed a victory sign. "So, let's beaver this thing."

***

Drenched in a cold sweat, I tugged mossy branches from the undergrowth, pine straw, anything I could carry. The Burning Tree might be gone, but every time I turned my back, I felt its eyes on me. Ancient. Angry. Or maybe that was just Charlotte's glare hitting everything in sight.

I threw my armload on a pile Curtis had already started. He could work when he wanted to, I had to give him that. Charlotte, on the other hand, was limping barefoot back and forth, carrying a few twigs at arm's length.

"You want to get this done, princess?" Curtis remarked. "Or you just collecting stuff to float downstream?"

"I'm not sacrificing my nails for nothing," she said, holding them out. Of course they were still flawless, like she'd just come out of a box. She was a waste of air, and when this was over, I'd make sure Drew knew it.

Curtis tipped his head to me. "Ellie's hanging in."

"That's because it's too late for her."

I turned my back, reaching for more branches, swallowing rage. All that mattered right now was that each load got us closer to Jean opening her eyes.

The sun hit noon, then midafternoon. By the time Curtis and I had collected what seemed like enough to clog the Amazon, my hands were bleeding, every breath scraped my raw lungs, and the shadows had lengthened into dusk. Curtis pointed to the old bed. "Okay, now we just have to clog the river up and it goes that direction. And then"—he hit a drum roll on his legs, grinning at Charlotte—"all hail the heroes of Bishop's Gap!"

"And then nothing," Charlotte informed him. "Like I've been saying, water going one way or the other won't make any difference, especially not to that." She pointed to the white clearing. "So let's just throw all this in the river and get out of here. I don't have a night to waste, even if you do."

"Yeah, but it's tricky." Curtis eyed the bank. "Right now, if we plug it up, it'll just make a lake."

He was right. "We have to clear the vines from the bed," I

said. "And the leaves. All the way down till the water can gain momentum."

Charlotte slumped against the pile of branches, setting off a flurry of ashes. "You've got to be kidding," she said, stifling a cough. "That much more?"

Curtis came over and ran a dirt-caked finger down her sleeve. "Just imagine how you'd feel if you'd done something, princess."

She slapped his hand away. "Touch me again, you're dead."

His wolf grin couldn't hide his fury. He was unraveling, drowning in Burning Tree ash.

Under the million leaf shadows, I pictured my hands around both their throats. To finally shut Curtis up. And pay Charlotte back for every whisper. Every insult. Everything she'd taken from me. For the way all the Levys looked at all the Casters. For taking Drew.

I took a step back. We had to get out. Now.

"It's getting too dark to work, anyway," I said. "We can finish up tomorrow."

"Guess it'll just be jerky and cream soda tonight," Curtis said, his eyes still fixed on Charlotte. "We'll meet back here soon as we wake up. With tools. Shovels, axes—got it?"

"Daybreak," said Charlotte.

Curtis laughed. "What?"

"Not when we wake up. That would be too long. Daybreak. Get this idiocy over with."

"So, you're counting the minutes till you see me again?" Curtis threw his arm around her shoulders.

She shoved him, hard. "Get *off* me." Then she took off through the woods faster than should have been possible barefoot.

We followed her golden wake through the mist until, at the

mouth of the woods, she turned. "Count to a thousand before you leave, both of you."

Curtis stopped. By now, it was so dark in the shadow of the trees, I couldn't read the look in his muddy eyes. "This some kind of test?" he said.

"Space," she said. "Personal Space. Here are the rules. We don't talk when we're not in the woods. We don't brush elbows. I don't know either of you out there, got it?"

"Got it?" she repeated, staring at Curtis.

He bowed with a flourish. "As you wish," he said, but his voice was taut.

As soon as they were both out of sight I broke into a run, heading for the fields, shaking off the dark vision of the woods. Curtis and Charlotte would self-destruct long before we finished anything. And we'd certainly worked together enough to fulfill Maggie's condition. More than enough. So, this was my chance to redeem myself. Open Jean's eyes. Tell her I was sorry.

Daybreak gave me exactly twelve hours to fix what I'd broken.

13

I WANTED TO RUN STRAIGHT FOR
Grandad's, raid his barn a second time for everything I'd need. But
first I had to make sure my parents wouldn't send the sheriff after
me, so I cut through the fields, then took Caster neighborhoods
toward the hospital, racking my brain for a believable reason to
be out all night. Nothing came. I couldn't think straight on these
deserted streets, all the marked houses looking out with blank
eyes, the flap of my shoes against pavement the only sound. The
truce hadn't broken while we were in the woods, but this kind
of silence meant it was holding on by a thread.

A few blocks from the hospital, I ran by Great-Aunt Ruby's
house with its round brick tower, its stained-glass windows
sparkling in the last rays of the setting sun like a fairytale plunked
into a beige-clapboard neighborhood. My great-aunt was sitting
on her back stoop, the only person I'd seen outside since leaving
the woods, her crimped red hair falling over her shoulders,
holding out a can of tuna to about a million cats. She had a
reputation for drawing people into never-ending conversations,
but when I tried to backtrack, she glanced up, her eyes sad to
their core. Then she blinked the gleam back into them. "Ellie,"
she beckoned, "come on in here. Sit a spell with me."

I'd never talked with the woman alone and I wasn't about to start now, especially with the twilight ticking away. "I'm sorry, Great-Aunt Ruby," I said. "I have to get back to the hospital."

"Of course you do." She adjusted the embroidered shawl that swept the porch steps. "But it's *Aunt* Ruby, you hear? *Great*'s for people fixing to keel over."

"Yes, ma'am."

"Now you go on and give my best to Jean," she said.

I winced. "Jean's not able to . . ."

"Oh, I'm well aware, dear," she interrupted. "I was in the woods, watching, remember, while your poor Daddy carved her name into that awful tree. But she needs all our best right now, wouldn't you agree? And as for not hearing us, I believe that's something only she can know." She craned her neck to peer over the fence at her neighbor's house. "Now, if you're not coming in, you best skedaddle. Those CDC people are everywhere."

So, Maggie had been right about that too. Aunt Ruby must have seen the panic on my face because she waved me off with a jeweled hand. "They just went next door, so I'd say you have some skittering time left."

She stood up, and it was only then I saw the mark on her door. Aunt Ruby lived with her sister, Gert. I hesitated. If Aunt Ruby was here, that meant . . .

"I'm sorry," I said, again, and this time I meant it. "About Great—about Aunt Gert."

"Well, thank you, but it's been her time for about a thousand years now. But not Jean's. And certainly not yours." She picked up her little dog, who was backing away from the horde of cats, and stuck him in her long bell sleeve. "Now, you ever need a listening ear, Ellie, you come on by, you hear?"

I nodded to placate her. I'd never need to talk that badly.

When I glanced back, she was standing with her head to one side, her eyes fixed on something in the distance. I definitely wouldn't be coming down this street again. But she'd given me an idea, and I practically flew the last few blocks to the hospital.

Inside, the corridors were as empty as the streets. Everyone must have packed into the rooms, crammed together on visitor's couches. The blaring announcements had stopped too, leaving the beeping of machines, and the soft hiss of whispers. I was almost to Jean's room when someone in a hazmat suit labeled *CDC* turned the corner toward me and I dodged into a closet marked "Staff," peering through the crack in the door till I was alone again. I couldn't afford another delay, not after wasting nearly a half hour getting here, but when I reached Jean's room, I had to stop again. A woman in the same CDC white stood in the middle of the room, facing away from me. I ducked back behind the door.

"And you say the symptoms first appeared on the morning of the twenty-first?"

"Yes," Dad's voice answered.

"As you know, Jean is patient zero. Can you account for all her activities in the previous few weeks?"

"She went to school," said Mom. "To her friends' houses. To the playground. No different from anyone else." Her voice held the now familiar edge.

"I'm not questioning that. We're simply trying to narrow down how this all started."

"Let her do her job, Arden," murmured Dad.

But neither of them were, not really. They obviously hadn't mentioned the mark on the door. Or the Burning Tree. Or the Levys. They were hiding, just like me, and in that moment, I felt closer to them than I had in years.

The conversation droned on, all about things that didn't matter. Jean's external appearance. The absence of symptoms. Then there was a click of heels, a pause at the door. "I'll be back in a few hours to monitor the progression. If you think of anything before then, you have my card."

I raced to the room next door, which was empty—if you didn't count the still figure on the bed. Our school janitor, Wilson Caster, lay with veins standing out on his face, his eyes vacant. I'd never seen him when he wasn't muttering *bunch of animals* and sweeping up trampled pizza in the cafeteria or scrubbing Silly String off the walls. This was the last place I wanted to be, staring at this man who couldn't look back, and as soon as the clipped footsteps disappeared down the hall, I hurtled out to Jean's room.

Under the grid lights, my sister's hair had lost some of its luster, and her face was paler—unless it wasn't the lights and she was worse. My heart skipped a beat as my parents turned to me. Mom let out her breath in relief. Then she crossed her arms and opened her mouth.

Before she or my dad could say anything, I burst out with, "Aunt Ruby asked if I could stay with her tonight."

"Ellie." Dad shook his head. "You ran off today. Again. How can we trust you to—"

I interrupted all the valid points he was about to make. "I know, and I'm really sorry. I was just—overwhelmed. But Aunt Ruby's alone now. I think she needs me. And I can't really do anything to help here."

Dad sighed. "Do you have any idea what it's like to tell a representative of the Centers for Disease Control and Prevention I have no idea where my other daughter is?"

"I'm sorry," I said again. "Really. I'm so sorry. I wasn't thinking straight."

Mom put an arm around me. "It was that Finch boy, wasn't it?" I nodded, willing the tears back, breathing in her familiar scent, lilac perfume and oil paint. She'd just given me the perfect out. And, in a way, she was actually right.

"Maybe it's best we let Ellie get a break from all this," Mom said, giving Dad her this-is-the-way-it's-going-to-be look.

Dad picked up the hospital phone and dialed out. "Hey, Aunt Ruby," he said after a moment. My face went hot. I should have realized this would be his obvious next step. And she would say she hadn't invited me, and I wouldn't be able to leave this room, stuck under total fluorescent supervision when I'd been so close to fixing everything. Just a river away. "Ellie just told us you've invited her to stay with you."

I held my breath as Aunt Ruby's rich voice poured through the receiver. Then a click, and Dad turned around. I continued to hold my breath, trying to read his face.

"She's waiting for you," he said, and my lungs started working again. Somehow, she'd understood. "But I want you to know I'll be checking up," he informed me. "Regularly. Everywhere you're supposed to be."

"I'll be there," I said, hoping it would be true.

Before I left, I made myself approach Jean. Close up, it was clear the change in her wasn't the lights. Everything but the blue of her veins was fading. I smoothed her hair, tucked the sheets in tighter. "Hey," I whispered. "I just wanted you to know . . . Aunt Ruby sends her best."

I watched for a flicker of expression, a twitch of the fingers. If the world held someone like Maggie, maybe Aunt Ruby was magic too. But of course, Jean didn't stir. *Hang on just one more night,* I thought. *Please, Jean. Don't leave before I make it right.*

———

I stood under the porch light at Aunt Ruby's door, staring at the random bits of stained glass above the knocker with no idea how to outmaneuver her. Just before I rapped on the door, she yanked it open like she'd been watching through the keyhole this whole time.

"So you're staying here, are you, Ellie?"

"Yes, ma'am. Thanks for letting me."

Her house smelled like peppermint and ferns. It was the ferns, I think, their familiar woodsy tang, that made me blurt out what I did. "Aunt Ruby, I promise I'll come back here soon, but . . ."

She pursed her lips. "But first you have to go into the woods."

"What? No. I just have to stop by Grandad's to straighten up some things."

Up and down the sidewalk, the streetlamps flicked on, time slipping through the holes in my plan.

"Before you go," she said, "let's get one thing straight. I will not stand in the way of anything but stupidity. Please have the courtesy to do the same. I smelled the woods on you this evening, and I know that look on your face. Heaven knows I've seen it often enough."

I was too shocked to say anything but "Yes, Aunt Ruby."

"Okay, then. I will cover for you until I can't," she said, and closed the door.

14

IN A FEVER OF HURRY, I SHOVELED leaves from the old riverbed, my shirt pulled up over my nose to shut out the searing air. Behind me, ash swirled where the Burning Tree had been, though everywhere else the woods held dead still, their darkness broken only by the rising crescent moon. That's all I needed, the shape of the mark hanging over my head—though maybe it was fitting I'd end the curse under that particular sliver of light.

By the time I'd cleared enough of the track to change the river's course, the crescent had cleared the top of the sky. Half the night gone. I grabbed the biggest branch from the pile by the river, dragged it to the bank, and managed to wrestle it halfway into the current before it refused to go farther. And I didn't hesitate—I jumped into the sharp chill of the Oakbend, fumbling with wet bark till I managed to jab the giant branch through underwater roots on the other side. By the time I'd gotten four branches in that way, my teeth chattered till my head ached, but the limbs crisscrossed into the web I'd pictured.

It took forever to weave the smaller branches in with numb hands. I had to keep ducking underwater to fix them in place, and each time I surfaced, thick algae water filled my ears, my nose, and rolled off my hair. But behind the dam, the water was rising.

Hours or minutes or maybe an eternity later, a trickle dropped into the old bed, into its ancient course, and I dove in one more time to plug the cracks that were left, feeling my way through the clinging silt at the bottom. On my way up, a forked branch caught my foot. I tried to yank it free, but the branches all shifted, pinning me underwater. *Don't panic,* I told myself, but five seconds passed. Ten. My lungs ached and I flailed, clawing branches, twigs, silt. Against all odds, I got a slippery handhold on a firm branch sticking out of the water, and in a moment, I was above the surface.

At first all I could do was gasp for air, choking on the ash. And I couldn't struggle completely free. Roots seemed to grow from under the bank, winding around my waist, holding me fast. The face of Mr. Finch, my eighth-grade science teacher, floated in front of me.

"Did you know you can succumb to hypothermia in sixty-degree water?" he'd said. "People who survived shipwrecks used to freeze to death waiting to be rescued—in the middle of summer."

I'd stopped listening then because I'd never be in a shipwreck. But this water was well below sixty degrees, and the moon was just halfway down the other side of the sky. By the time anyone found me, it would be too late.

I stuck my arms through the mess of roots and braced my head above water, staring at the ghosts that whirled through the clearing until the river warmed, until the charred air faded and all I could smell was notebook paper.

I floated through a paper universe, dodging crisp blue lines straight to Drew. He was with me, I knew it, because the world suddenly made sense. This was how it should be. This was how it should always be. Then he dropped away, and I sank into a cloud of fresh-breeze detergent.

Branches grabbed at my feet, and I tried to jerk back. My legs wouldn't work. Shouting wouldn't come, either, like the dreams where you can't move and you can't run and you can't wake up.

"She's freezing. We have to get her warm." Drew's voice echoed from a galaxy away. "That's your department, Charlotte."

"And how exactly am I supposed to do that? I don't thaw people."

Her voice forced my eyes open to a blurry room, and I couldn't get myself to think why Drew and Charlotte and Curtis would all be standing there, pale as ice.

I must have imagined the relief crossing Charlotte's face because the first words out of her mouth were, "That was so stupid, Ellie. Going in there alone." She propped a pillow behind my head. "Stupid."

"Not the time," Drew said, bending close to peer into my eyes, his face tight with concern. He smelled like safety and ivory soap. "You okay, Ellie?"

"I'm fine," I wanted to say. "Perfectly fine." But since I still couldn't get the words out, I probably wasn't, and their faces disappeared into heaviness again.

I don't know how long I was out before the weight turned into blankets. The blur cleared to Drew's World Series pennant on the wall at the foot of the bed, the old greats postered around it. Joe and Mickey and Babe on the navy walls, everything like always in this room I loved. Weak sunlight streamed through the windows, so somehow, I'd survived the night.

"She's still shaking." Drew layered on another blanket. "This isn't enough. Ideas?"

I didn't mind the shivering, not cocooned in here where everything was right between Drew and me again. Only I couldn't catch his eye with Charlotte in the room, her hair falling in soft waves over her shoulders, looking down at me like I was some kind of waterborne virus. She had nothing to be jealous of now. My own hair hung stringy in my face, and I raised my half-ton hand far enough to push it back. Not that it would make much of a difference. I was probably a mess of scratches and river mud.

Curtis grinned. "Well, there's always the microwave."

"Ha, ha," I whispered, my voice sounding as weak as I felt.

"I was thinking more along the lines of a hot shower," Drew said.

Yes. That's exactly what I needed to warm me up enough to breathe and head back to the river. Fifteen more minutes of work in the woods and I'd be done. I managed to get my feet over the side of the bed, but when I tried to stand, my legs buckled. Curtis and Drew had to help me over brown carpet and then white tile, till I clutched at the shower door.

"Okay, Charlotte," Drew called over his shoulder as Curtis walked out to the hall, wiping mud off his sleeves. "Your turn."

But I wasn't about to let Charlotte Levy help me. She'd tell it all over school, and she'd twist it somehow, make it something I couldn't live down.

"I can do it," I said. "And then I'll be out of here, I promise. You can have your house back."

"Listen," Drew said, his arm strong around my shoulders. "I don't know what you're playing at—they won't tell me—but whatever it is, you could have died."

"But I didn't," I said, trying to keep my teeth from chattering. "Thanks to you."

Drew turned me to face him, still holding me up, and for once in my life I couldn't read his expression. "Things are really bad here, Ellie. They can't get worse. You understand?"

"You're saying I'm going to make them worse?" Even through the aching cold, the back of my throat began to burn.

His eyes didn't leave mine. "Maybe. Yeah."

"I had to do it, Drew. All of it. You have to believe—"

He didn't let me finish. "See, what I can't figure out is, you were pretty sure you'd never be in the woods at the same time as Charlotte. Remember that? And yet, this morning, there you were—together."

"Listen, I didn't have a choice. Really. I just can't—"

"You can't tell me why." His jaw clenched, and suddenly he was a thousand miles away. Tears pricked my eyes, but I couldn't cry, not right there in front of him. I withdrew, grabbing at the shower door.

He let out a long breath. "I'll set out a towel."

Once the door shut behind him, I fumbled with my clothes. Then I stood under the shower head with the faucet cranked to "H." The ache that stung deep through my bones pulled me fully awake. The others must have found me at daybreak, and they'd brought me here because Drew's house was closest. Or maybe Charlotte just wanted to make a point.

I watched mud slide from my bruised legs.

"Drew found you some clothes," Charlotte called through the

door when I turned off the water. "I'll throw them in. And Ellie, we don't have all day."

A blue sweater set and a long jean skirt landed on the bathroom counter. His mom's. I put them on and ran my fingers through my hair in the foggy mirror.

Curtis whistled when I limped down the green-carpeted stairs to the kitchen, holding my wet clothes. "Check out Miss Bishop's Gap 1980." He held a waffle in each hand, both half-eaten.

I ignored him. And I ignored Charlotte slipping her arm through Drew's like she owned him.

"Sorry for—all of this," I said. "I'll get the clothes back soon as I can."

That used to be all it would take to bring Drew's grin back after we fought, an apology. Then he'd sling an arm around me, and we'd be closer than before. But not this time. I tried again. "Or earlier. First period. Before your mom notices."

Drew slipped his arm out of Charlotte's and turned to the sink. "Yeah. She's not really in a position to do that."

Until that second, I hadn't given a thought to the mark that must be on Drew's door too. I'd stood face-to-face with him in the hospital cafeteria and hadn't asked why he was there, who he'd lost. I'd lied to him, and then I'd run off.

But there wasn't an ounce of surprise on Charlotte's face. My stomach dropped. He'd told her about his mom and hadn't said a word to me. Or maybe she'd remembered to ask.

Curtis grabbed another waffle from the stack on the counter. "This is a little awkward. I don't really do awkward."

"Oh, come on," Charlotte said. "That's all you do." She rubbed her hand on Drew's plaid flannel sleeve.

Curtis gagged, loudly, and I didn't blame him.

"We'd better go," I said, trying to get Drew to look at me, see

how sorry I really was. "Thanks for the rescue. For everything."
He nodded, his head down.

We were almost out the door, my feet flopping around in his mom's shoes, when he grabbed my elbow, halting me, and stuck a Styrofoam cup of something hot in my hand. "Don't burn anything else down," he murmured. "And please don't drown."

So, he did still care. Just like that, I stopped shaking. "I'm going to help your mom, Drew," I promised.

He stepped back, hands up. "I don't want to hear it. Okay? The damage is already done. If you're smart, you'll stay away."

"I can't. If you knew—"

But he'd already shut the door.

15

I WANTED TO BANG ON THE DOOR, make Drew believe me, but nothing would change until he saw the remedy for himself. Instead, I quickened my pace to catch up with Curtis and Charlotte, already on the main road back to the woods. I'd been so close to finishing alone. My legs ached where the branches had snagged me, and the cup of cocoa sloshed over my scratched-up hand, but we didn't have any more time to waste.

When I reached them, Charlotte checked her watch. "Okay, so it's almost eight. Finishing at daybreak obviously isn't going to happen, thanks to Ellie."

"Hey, it's not like you were helping," I told her.

They both turned to stare at me. "Really," Charlotte said, pulling ChapStick from her purse and gliding it on while Curtis watched like it was a show just for him. "The point was, we were supposed to go in *together*."

"We did go in together. And it wasn't working. You know that as well as I do."

Charlotte snapped the pink tube shut. "So what, you thought you'd sabotage everything we did yesterday?"

I bit off the urge to remind her, once again, that she'd done absolutely nothing. "Of course not. My sister's sick. And my grandad."

"Then what?" She crossed her arms like she'd done at every lunch table since kindergarten. "Never mind. I get it. You're the Caster who's going to save them all, aren't you? So, you can't work with a Levy, and Finches aren't good enough."

I turned to Curtis, the only one who might possibly give me the benefit of the doubt. "Look, I couldn't sleep, and I couldn't stay away." That was true as far as it went, but from the looks on their faces, it wasn't enough. "I'm sorry, okay? And thanks for fishing me out. Both of you."

Curtis took a dramatic bow, flashing that wolf grin. "We're here to serve."

"Anyway," Charlotte said, starting off again like I hadn't groveled, "do we go to class, or do we skip?"

I ran up next to her. "Wait, they opened school?" Even for Bishop's Gap that seemed impossibly resilient.

"Yeah." Curtis passed us, jogging backwards on his toes. "See, apparently the youth of this fine town need something productive to do while everybody dies. The hospital is way overcrowded—so, theory is, school will keep us out of trouble."

"Because that worked so well before," Charlotte muttered, tossing her hair. "The point is, do we skip?"

"We don't have to," I said. "I was almost done. We just have to stick in a few more branches—we'll barely be tardy."

"About that," Curtis said, scratching his tangled hair, "I don't know what exactly you tried last night, but all the branches we'd piled up were gone. They weren't in the river, either. Just the ones holding you down. The rest of it must have floated away."

A flush crept up my face. I'd done it again, made things worse for nothing. And they both knew it.

Charlotte opened her mouth, but before she could twist the knife, Curtis pointed at the first set of stores along the road. "Whoa," he said. "Get a look at that."

Nothing was different at Caster Tackle and Ammo, but a huge sign plastered the windows of Levy Sports Supply.

LEVYS ONLY.
IN THE INTEREST OF PUBLIC HEALTH.

My heart froze. The Levys had just stepped over the line. Broken the truce.

Charlotte shrugged. "You can't blame them. Everyone knows a Caster did this." She looked at me, and there was nothing I could say. After all, she'd seen the Tree. "So, we skip?" she asked again.

Of course that's what we should do. My sister was worse, and the Levys had just pulled the pin on Bishop's Gap.

Curtis cracked his knuckles. "So, I have what you might call expertise in this area. Rules of pulling it off. One. Get your names on the roll. Two. Don't leave at the same time. I'll get stomach pain first period. Charlotte, you get the kind of headache where you see bursts of light during second. And Ellie . . ."

And at that second, I realized why it wouldn't work. "I can't," I said. "My dad's going to call to check up on me. I don't know when. If I'm not where I'm supposed to be, he'll call the sheriff. They'll all go straight to the woods."

"We'll get it done without you then," said Curtis blithely. "You can be there for the ribbon cutting."

Charlotte huffed. "Does no one else here understand what *together* means? We'll just have to wait until after school. Hope everyone lasts that long, Ellie."

A sharp retort died on my lips. I hated to waste another second with Jean's time ticking off the clock, but Aunt Ruby couldn't cover for me forever. If we got caught in the woods, everything would be over.

I stopped so fast, one of the oversized shoes slid off. Aunt Ruby. By now she'd have to know I'd been out all night. I had to reach her before she called Dad.

Again, Aunt Ruby pulled the door open before I had a chance to knock. Behind her, the smell of bacon wafted out, and I suddenly realized I was starving.

"Oh, my," she said, her mouth twitching. "Overnight, it seems you aged . . . and then you shrank."

"I'm sorry I didn't come—"

She held up a hand. "I don't want to hear it."

So, she'd already talked to Dad, which meant our chance was gone. He wouldn't let me out of his sight again. Right there on her doorstep, I came completely undone, didn't even try to stop the tears.

Her face softened. "You'd best come in."

I stepped into a room dancing with fern shadows, wiping my face and trying to hide my limp.

"Well, one thing is perfectly clear," she said. "You can't go to school like that."

"It's all I have." My only change of clothes was still sopping wet.

She narrowed her eyes. "Hmm . . . the opera one, I think."

There was no time to wonder what she meant. "What did you tell him?"

"Tell whom, dear?"

"Dad."

Aunt Ruby's fluffball dog ran up, toenails clicking on the polished floor, and growled at my shoes.

"Banquo," she said, "be polite. Now, about your father—when he called yesterday evening, I told him you were settled for the night. I assume that was true, yes? He hasn't called again, not yet. It looks to me like you didn't hold up your end of the deal on avoiding stupidity, but I suppose it's too late to stop you now."

"Thank you," I managed to whisper, warmth creeping back through the ache in my chest. For some reason, Aunt Ruby still trusted me.

She tapped on her lips with a scarlet nail. "Yes, definitely the opera one. Come, Banquo."

The dog skittered over to her, yipping, and she swept out of the hall. I followed the whiff of bacon and eggs to the next room, where swatches of light from a peacock stained-glass window fell across a dining room table. It was set for two with china and silver serving bowls. She'd been expecting me long before this.

She clattered back in then, holding out a black dress with a deep V-neck front. "Here you are, dear. It is perhaps a trifle formal for school but," she sighed, "anything would be better than what you currently have hanging on your bones."

My eyes went wide. "Aunt Ruby," I choked, "I can't wear this."

"Go on, now." She waved a dismissive hand. "Change."

In her tiny first-floor powder room, I slipped the dress over my head. From what I could see in the wavy mirror, it actually wasn't a disaster. Windblown hair fell over my shoulders, and my eyes shone hazel above the dark fabric, just like Jean had always described me. And for once I didn't look like I'd outgrown myself.

Aunt Ruby blinked when I walked out. "I suppose that'll tide you over for today." She held out a pair of beaded flats. "Slip those on. What should we do with those rags you walked in here with? Burn them?"

"No," I said, feeling a smile take over my face. I couldn't remember the last time that happened. "I have to give them back."

"Pity," said Aunt Ruby, handing me a napkin with two slices of bacon. "Skedaddle, now. You best get on to school."

But I had to get something right this morning, after letting down Jean and Drew and Aunt Ruby and pretty much everyone else. "Could I just use your phone first?"

When Dad picked up, I took a deep breath. "Hey," I said. "I'm—I'm checking in."

"Is Aunt Ruby there?"

"Ha-loo," she warbled over my shoulder.

I had to know. "How's Jean?"

On Dad's end, the receiver rustled. He was probably looking over at her. "Oh, she's—she's the same as she's been."

But she hadn't been the same last night, and I could only guess she was worse now. Maybe he wouldn't let himself see it.

"Okay," I said. "Good. I'll be at school if you need me." And *I love you*, I wanted to say. *I love you and Mom and Jean.* But the words stuck in my throat, lost in whatever made me mess things up again and again.

I wanted to rush straight to the hospital, to Jean, but I couldn't spend the day watching her fade. I had to get through the hours at Bishop's Gap High.

16

EVERY LEVY STORE I PASSED ON the way had the *LEVYS ONLY* sign taped to a window, but there was no hint of Caster retaliation. Not yet. *Just a few more hours. Just hold off until we can finish.* At least we could still buy groceries and gasoline.

When I got to Bishop's Gap High, all columns and bricks and flying buttresses, the type of building designed to make people rise to the occasion, no one was lingering outside. The first bell rang as I took the broad granite steps two at a time. Inside, sheets of charcoal-sketched hands from art class fluttered out as I hurried through the empty halls. Gum wrappers and paper scraps stirred along the walls, for all the world like I was the only one here, trespassing in my own school on a Tuesday morning.

I passed three classrooms with dark windows before I tried the door on mine. It opened to a room of silent faces, some from other sections, the desks all crammed together. They hadn't put our families into separate classes yet. Like always, the Levys sat closest to the windows. Casters crowded by the door, the Finches a buffer between us. Up front, Ms. Levy was scribbling something in a notebook, and she didn't glance up even when the late bell rang. Her bleached hair, normally waved to perfection, hung flat, and she wasn't wearing makeup.

So, this was what it looked like when the world slipped off the edge.

Drew was nowhere to be seen, but in the back row, Charlotte raised an eyebrow at my dress. I couldn't tell if the look on her face was envy or contempt, but it didn't really matter either way. I found a desk on the front row with an empty seat next to it, so when Drew finally came in, we'd have to talk. And I could tell him again how sorry I was.

He still wasn't there when the PA system squealed on. "Good morning, students." That was the flat voice of our vice-principal. She never did the announcements, just sat in her office reading gray files and sipping endless cups of oolong tea. "As you can see, we've had to make some modifications with our town's current . . . situation. We appreciate your cooperation as we sort things out."

When the announcements ended, saying that pretty much everything except birthdays had been canceled, no one stirred. And Drew still hadn't come. With every jerk of the clock's second hand, my heart thudded faster, and I pushed down the panic that something had happened to him too. I couldn't bear one more thing.

Ms. Levy continued to scribble in the dead quiet of the room. "Take out your notebooks," she finally said, looking up at the Levys like the rest of us didn't exist, "and sketch—oh, I don't care. Draw whatever you want."

Shuffling filled the room. I pulled out my dogeared composition notebook and flipped past all the sketches of the aspen sisters, drawing after drawing, like Monet's haystacks: morning, afternoon, night, different shades of silver in their cracking bark. But they were closed off to me now. I searched for some other image, something else to think about, to cling to, but all that rushed in was being caught by those branches, held underwater. When I shook that picture away, I saw the veins branching out on Jean's face. On Grandad's.

All around me number twos scratched across paper, everyone fighting the same images of the people they loved. Or giving in, maybe, filling their pages with evidence of what I'd done. When Ms. Levy finally called time, I found I'd sketched something after all—Jean's initials, deep through the paper, exactly as Dad had etched them into the Burning Tree. Which was exactly right—just a few more hours and she'd be free.

Halfway into second period, Drew walked through the door, but he didn't even glance at the empty desk next to me, just handed Ms. Levy a note and took a seat across the room. That should have warned me, sitting alone in a packed classroom. Still, on the way to lunch, I caught up with him.

"Drew."

He turned, took one look at my dress, and his face closed down.

I went on anyway. "I just wanted to say, you know, thanks for the cocoa. It helped."

"No problem. You okay now?"

I nodded. "Just waterlogged."

"Good," he said, and that was all, like I was someone he barely knew.

The school was thawing out now, little pockets of conversation opening up on the Caster and Levy sides of the halls. Drew turned to go, but I couldn't let him.

"Is—is everything okay with your mom?"

He swallowed hard. "I think she's the same. It's not easy to tell, you know?"

I nodded. "I just thought—I mean, I was wondering if you came in late because of her—or—you know, if something else happened."

"No, nothing else."

I waited for him to say something more, my heart racing. And then he did. "Look, Ellie, I can't do this, okay? I can't watch you—whatever it is you're trying. I'm sorry. I can't."

While I stood there, frozen, he called, "Hey, Stevens," over my head and went past me to a group I'd been in class with all my life but still didn't really know.

And just like that, we weren't friends—or enemies. We weren't anything anymore.

The afternoon stretched out, endless. There weren't enough teachers to change classes, so we stayed packed together, everyone on edge. Ms. Levy had wilted, her face sagging into wrinkles as she held up our anthropology textbook. "Where are you in this?" When no one answered, she shook her head. "Just read whatever you think you're supposed to."

Drew sat two rows over and about a million miles away. I shifted to keep him out of my peripheral vision as I thumbed through the pages, yearning for this last hour to be over so Charlotte and Curtis and I could escape to the woods. I didn't care who got the credit for fixing our town anymore as long as we finished the task. Because the more I thought about last night, the tighter my stomach twisted. I hadn't imagined those branches trapping me, the roots winding around my legs. I hadn't imagined the swirling ash. And all my work hadn't floated down the river on its own. Something in there was fighting us back.

My fingers stopped at a familiar page. Ancient Myths and Rituals.

You've been looking in the wrong section, Maggie had said. *Not botany. Myths.*

There wouldn't be anything about Bishop's Gap in a textbook, but at least checking into this portion would be something to do. I flipped through bright gods drinking nectar on Olympus, Gilgamesh wrestling his way through the world, and Odysseus yearning for home until the worn pages gave way to crisp ones, pages that were never assigned, lesser myths teachers ran out of time for each year.

A sidebar stopped me dead, a plain line drawing of people bowing to a massive tree. *A common motif in many ancient cultures, the World Tree was viewed as a bridge between earth and heaven*, the text read. *Often portrayed as an ash, many ash trees became sites of sacrifice.*

An ash. Just like the Burning Tree. A chill prickled my scalp as I read on. *Some believed the World Tree bestowed runes, symbols of power.*

Underneath, they'd included a list, dozens of ancient runes and what they'd meant. And there, buried halfway down the page, was the mark. Our mark. The one on every door in this town. I traced the dotted line across to its meaning. *Calamity.*

I slammed the book shut, grabbed my backpack, and rushed to the front of the room, clutching my stomach. Ms. Levy barely looked up.

"I need to be excused, please. Something I ate."

She leaned away, waving me off. At the door, I glanced back. Drew had his head down like almost everyone else, but Charlotte was glaring daggers at me. "Meet you there," I mouthed. Then I took off past the bathroom and out the front door.

When Dad called, Ms. Levy would cover for me. And I had to get out of that room, because if the World Tree was real, and if I'd just burned it down, there was only one place to go.

I burst through the door at Blooms where the coffee smell had grown too strong. Light from the hanging lamps reflected off the aqua floor in unsteady patterns, and Maggie stood behind the counter in the same blue dress, calm as before. "Hello, Ellie. What'll it be?"

I opened the book to the World Tree page and thumped it down in front of her.

Her expression didn't change. "Very good," she said.

"Good? You're telling me I just burned down some kind of bridge-to-heaven tree?"

She smiled, her brown eyes glinting. "Not exactly."

My knees went wobbly, and I grabbed for the closest chair. Maggie set a glass of water in front of me. "Drink that down," she said, taking a seat on the other side of the white table.

When I'd drained it, she took a sip from her endless cup of coffee. "You didn't burn the World Tree because that Tree is bigger than this cosmos," she said, matter-of-fact, like she'd just explained the menu. "It connects everything. All places. All worlds."

She wasn't helping. Apparently, there wasn't just a World Tree, there was a Universe Tree, and I'd brought its anger down on all of us.

Her voice had gone singsong now. "It draws its water from the well of memory. All knowledge flows through its branches."

"Maggie," I said, clutching at my water glass like it could hold me up, "I don't know what that means."

But she had that look on her face again, like she'd forgotten I was there, reciting something that couldn't be interrupted. "The stars you see at night hang from its roots. If you could get beyond them, break past the universe, you would reach its trunk, and if you pulled yourself up, hand-over-hand through the worlds, you would come out into great green leaves."

"Tell me"—I was nearly yelling now—"what did I do to it?"

Maggie's eyes finally focused on mine. "Nothing," she said. "I told you. No human could burn the World Tree."

I slumped back against the chair, still processing that she'd said *human* like she wasn't one, when she went on. "But its seeds were scattered once, long ago. I think you'd call it *once upon a time*." She looked out the window at our ashy air and I held my breath, though I knew exactly what came next. "One fell here."

I didn't want any of that to make sense, and I definitely didn't want to live in a world where old stories could fall into your backyard and grow a mythic tree. But wasn't that exactly what Jeremiah Levy had called it? *The tree that held up the sky.* The room reeled, spots sparking in front of my eyes.

I didn't see Maggie get up, but suddenly she was setting a peanut butter and jelly sandwich sliced into four triangles in front of me. "Eat that," she commanded.

I nibbled at the crust, its familiar comfort of salt and grape jelly, until the room slowed down. "So why did our Tree . . . change?"

"Its knowledge grew," she answered. "And its power. Just like the Tree it came from."

"And when I burned it down . . ." I couldn't finish the thought. I had absolutely no idea what to say.

"You released it," Maggie finished for me.

I'd known that, really, since I'd stood in that clearing and witnessed the emptiness. I'd released a power I couldn't begin to understand. I pushed away the rest of the crusts, my stomach churning. "But if I put the river back, that fixes everything?"

"That will be up to you," she said. "But there won't be a second chance." She pulled the book from the counter and pointed to the rune that marked our doors. "This one is more than calamity."

I could have told her that. Calamity didn't begin to cover it.

"It means the moon," she said. "And moons wane. Yours is pulling the sick out like the tide."

Last night, the moon had been a sliver in the sky. I swallowed. "Then, tomorrow night, when it's gone?"

She nodded. "They'll go with it."

So we had another night. But just one more.

"Maggie," I whispered. "How do you know this?"

Across the table, she began to shimmer, and it wasn't a trick of the light. She'd gone suddenly translucent. "I came with the seed," she said, her voice a current rushing from everywhere at once. "I am the water it carried from the well. I am Memory. I stay with the tree. I stay with the river. I do not forget."

I blinked and she was solid again, stirring her coffee like nothing had happened, which could only mean I was losing my mind.

"So, I see what has been," she said, her voice back to normal. "I remember. And no one like you has come in here before, Ellie." She reached across the table and laid her hand on mine, cool and completely smooth and very real. "You are capable of this—moving the river, setting things right. Just not by yourself."

I nodded, my hands shaking as I put the book into my backpack. This was beyond anything I'd bargained for. But I had the answer to our town now. And I understood why she'd said *together*. One person couldn't go up against a Tree like that, even if it had just been reduced to ash.

"Now you must remember"—her eyes were on mine as I stood up—"the tree gathered knowledge. It became what it knew."

And I'd seen exactly what it had become. The Levys betrayed us—and so it betrayed everyone.

Maggie was still watching as I stepped out into a world where somewhere above our smoke-filled sky, a golden Tree soared through space, through all the worlds. Our town finally made sense. And for the first time since the mark hit our door, I didn't feel alone. I knew what we faced.

It was time to get my sister back.

17

EVEN WITH HELP, I COULDN'T move a river in an opera dress. I made it to Aunt Ruby's house just as school let out, where the tower and glittering stained glass fit right into a world connected to everything else by a golden Tree. Inside, though, the rooms still smelled faintly of bacon, which brought me right back to earth, back to Bishop's Gap where in our hospital everyone was dying.

After I changed, I called Dad, buying time before he checked up on me again. The gold-rimmed hall clock had ticked around to just after four.

"You doing okay?" he said, his voice anxious. "When I called, the school told me you weren't well."

"Oh, it was just bad chicken or something," I said. "I'm fine, now. Really."

"Good." It was only one syllable, but I could feel his relief though the line.

"So, I'm just going to finish things up here," I said, biting my lip over the lie. "I'll see you tonight."

On my way out the door, I slipped on my sneakers. They'd be with me to finish what I'd started. Now I just had to hold Curtis and Charlotte together, fight off the Burning Tree, and move the river before the moon waned away.

It was only when I arrived at the gravel lot by the woods that I realized my mistake. The sheriff's car and an unfamiliar black sedan were parked by the entrance. My seared red shoes stood out like cardinals, evidence of what I'd done.

Before I had time to think, Charlotte stepped out from the trees, gesturing me over. I quickly scuffed my sneakers up the best I could, hoping dirt would cover all the scorch marks, then dashed into the cover of the woods, crossing over into myth. Ashy air filled my nose and mouth, the bitter taste seeping down my throat. Charlotte and Curtis both hunched behind a piney screen. He looked right at home, but her face was whiter than the ash that floated around us. "Where have you been?" she hissed.

I couldn't tell them about the World Tree, or the seed that fell here, or how her family had twisted it into the Burning Tree. They'd think I was crazy, and it didn't change what we had to do.

"Bad chicken," I whispered back.

Curtis's glance fell to my singed sneakers where the dirt hadn't masked anything. "Bonfire at my Grandad's," I said in a hushed voice. "A few weeks ago. It got a little out of control."

Charlotte gazed around at all the floating ash. "Oh, you think?"

Fear stabbed down my spine. The burned sneakers on their own didn't prove anything, but they were another strike against me. Against my family.

"Bonfire. Right," Curtis mouthed. "So do we wait?" He pointed to the cars. "Or risk it?"

Neither of us had time to answer before muffled voices came through the trees, heading our way. Curtis put a hand on both our backs and pushed us to the cindery ground. I had to give him credit for stealth when it mattered, though he'd obviously been eating Funyuns, which took most of the credit back.

Footsteps crunched on the pine needle path a few feet away. "Looks like arson all right." I froze. That was Sheriff Caster.

A woman's voice answered, the one I'd heard in Jean's room the night before. "Possibly, it released a fungus of some sort when it burned. The spores affected those with underlying respiratory issues first."

"Certainly, it points to something in the air," a second man said, his voice brittle and sure.

When car doors finally slammed, Curtis and Charlotte pushed to their feet, but I couldn't move, rooted to the spot in my damaged shoes, that man's words ringing in my ears. *Something in the air.* Spores hadn't made people sick. I knew that, but still, I couldn't get that phrase out of my head. It drowned out everything else, even the fear they'd trace the arson back to me.

Charlotte tapped me on the shoulder. "Are you coming?" she whispered. "Or have you decided to do everyone a favor and turn yourself in?"

I stood, stretching the ache from my bruised legs, hating for the millionth time that Charlotte had to be the one to walk into Maggie's café with me. There was no point in answering, so we all crept wordlessly to the river. Even Curtis didn't break a single twig—all of us probably afraid of what could happen, who we could become in here.

When we made it past the clearing to the river, only two branches still stood upright in the current, which was just as well. It meant the sheriff hadn't noticed any activity here.

All afternoon, Charlotte merely teetered back and forth again with twigs while I gathered limbs from deeper in the woods. I could barely drag them out, my muscles like water now, but

Curtis drove them across the river and into the other bank like they weighed nothing.

"Okay," he said as the first water spilled into the old riverbed. "We can fill this in with the smaller ones now."

We plugged the holes with the twigs and then with rocks. By late afternoon, even Charlotte was really helping, handing me stones from farther up the bank. The first shine of water had turned to a gush, washing down the bend and out of sight. No one had to go underwater. No one was caught by roots. And no one was talking, too exhausted and maybe too afraid the sheriff would come back and hear us.

I'd expected the woods to put up more of a fight, but maybe this was why Maggie had said we had to work together. Maybe the three of us had staved it off.

By dusk, the gush had turned to a torrent. We plugged the last holes with moss, pebbles, anything we could find in a race against the dark. And just as the sun went down, our dam held. The old track surged with water and overran its shallow banks. I held my breath, waiting for the beautiful thing, some mythic sign the curse was over.

"Yes!" Curtis shouted, fist-pumping into the sunset. "Behold, the river-benders!" He looked around. "Though I thought there'd be more to it. Some kind of cosmic boom or something."

I knew exactly how he felt.

"Keep your voice down," Charlotte whispered. "Do you really want someone to come in here and move everything back?"

He grinned at her. "Thought you didn't believe in this, princess."

She tossed her head. "I don't. Not before the proof."

And, just like that, the weight of Bishop's Gap flew off my shoulders. The beautiful thing, the proof—that was happening somewhere else. My sister opening her eyes. "We have to get to town," I told them. Just a few minutes more, and I could tell Jean everything. Then I'd tear those signs off all the windows.

"Hey," said Curtis. "What's that?"

Where the river had been, ashy ground sucked down the last of the water, drying into lizard-skin cracks. And from the parched dirt, something white reached up.

The white thing became a row of curved points. I tried to scream, but the wood wrapped its fingers around my mouth.

Curtis made for the old bed like it was the end zone and he'd just been released from the huddle, like all the signs weren't shouting *stay back*. He clambered down the bank at full speed, clods of dry dirt spraying out behind him, then stooped to get a closer look. Then he bolted upright. "It's a hand. Was, I mean. Just bone now."

I still couldn't scream, but I didn't have to. Charlotte did it for me. The echo of her shriek sent the birds to cawing all through the long shadows of the trees. I'd forgotten they were there, the woods had been silent so long. There was a rustling in the underbrush.

Curtis snapped a root from the dry bank. "That's creepy. Super creepy."

A rush of acid stung my throat. Maybe this was why moving the river had been so easy. The forest wanted us to see this, trap us here, which meant everything could all still fall apart.

"We have to go." I could finally speak. "Someone had to have heard Charlotte. They can't find us here."

"That's for sure. They'll think vandalism," Curtis agreed. But instead of moving, he poked around with the root. "But . . . I kind of want to know what else is down here."

Charlotte hadn't made a move to leave, either.

"That's nothing to do with us," I insisted, trying to believe it.

Curtis bent and brushed at the ground. Then he whistled. "Yep, that's a body." He looked up as dirt slid away from an arm, a ribcage. "Looks like we've got something cosmic going on here after all."

I sank to my knees in the scratchy river grass that smelled of earthworms. Every step to fix this took me farther in, right to the heart of the haunting. Because now I knew exactly what the Burning Tree remembered.

It wasn't just the fire. It was Benjamin Caster, who'd lost his wife and baby in that burning cabin. He'd been lying here all this time, right at the roots of the Burning Tree, where Jeremiah Levy offed him and buried him and then moved the river to hide what he'd done.

Curtis hoisted himself up to the bank, then wiped his hands on his pants. "So, who do you think that is?"

Before I could tell him, Charlotte stalked over, her eyes gleaming in the last of the cloudy light. "That's Jeremiah Levy."

Rage flashed through me, so complete the air should have ignited. I jumped to my feet. "That's a Caster and you know it."

"You mean a Caster killed him for something he didn't do," she retorted, and I saw her face, the whole world, through a blur of red.

Curtis watched us, bemused. "Cosmic. Like I said."

I whirled toward him. "Stay out of this."

He held his hands up in mock surrender. "Got it. Finches don't count."

Charlotte was already kicking little clods of dirt over the bank and onto the bones. Of course she wanted to push all this back under the river. It was proof of what the Levys had done.

"You can't just walk away from this," I said.

She didn't even glance my way. "Watch me."

Curtis picked up the purse Charlotte had dropped by the edge of the clearing, brushed ash and moss off it and held it out. "Hey, I'm all for staying here all night, getting caught with a skeleton and a burned-down tree, but maybe we should see if everyone got well."

Charlotte grabbed the purse. "Fine," she snapped. "Let's go find out what didn't happen."

18

WE RACED FOR THE HOSPITAL IN the last of the light, even Charlotte. And when we got to the first house past the woods, I stopped dead. We all did, because on the door of that house, the mark of the crescent moon had faded like someone had just bleached it out. And it wasn't only on that door. Every mark in sight was fading. Relief washed over me. Jean was going to be okay. Everybody was. Moving the river had actually put the Burning Tree to rest.

"No way," Curtis said, rubbing at a fever blister. "That worked?"

Charlotte stared at me, her eyes huge. Then she threw her arms around me like we hadn't just found buried bones. Like, for that moment, Levy and Caster didn't matter. She stepped back just as quick, but with that one touch, everything had changed. No more standing outside looking in.

After that, I didn't even feel the pavement under my feet until we reached the hospital. The *LEVYS ONLY* signs on the windows blurred into nothing as we ran by them. But the hospital parking lot was still packed and silent, no one celebrating a sudden miraculous wave of remedy.

"You know," Curtis commented, "this doesn't look right if everyone's gotten well."

"Shut up," I said, but dread set in as we walked into the blue-lit halls. Charlotte clattered down the first corridor to the left and Curtis slouched down the next one, his hands in his pockets. As soon as he disappeared around the corner, I peeked into a Caster room, afraid of what I'd find, and I didn't last more than a second before I ran back out of the hospital, trying to forget the ruined face I'd seen, the veins across it purply dark. Moving the river hadn't worked—all that hope and lugging branches and almost drowning was for nothing. All we'd done was fade the marks on the doors.

Outside, a fingernail moon hung over my head, the last moon Jean would get. Anger blistered through me. Maggie had promised by now she'd be okay. I took off for Blooms like I hadn't been hauling branches all afternoon. Past the parking lot, Charlotte blazed up with Curtis right on her sparkling pink heels. I'd never seen his face so pale. Never seen anyone's face that pale.

"I'm done with no answers." Charlotte spat the words at me. "Done."

"Same," I said, barely believing the words coming out of my mouth. "I'm with you."

Curtis pulled me back, spun me around.

"Hey!" I swatted at him. "Let me go!"

In front of us, Charlotte didn't break stride. Curtis dug his fingers deep into my arm. "Did you see what those people looked like back there? Did you see them?" His voice pitched high and he reeked of Funyuns and grief. "They looked worse. Why are they worse, Ellie?"

"How should I know?" I wasn't about to tell him they were

waning with the moon. That would push him straight over the edge, and right now, he'd take me with him. Just when I'd started to let my guard down.

He released my arm, shaking. "Sorry," he muttered. "Really. I'm sorry." He forced a lopsided grin. "I didn't get my Red Vines fix today."

An engine hummed down a side street, headed our way, and I stepped out of his reach, fumbling for an answer that would satisfy him. "Look, we have to get to Maggie. She'll explain everything. Maybe it'll take some time. Maybe the marks go first, and then . . . everyone wakes up."

I only said it to calm him down, but still my hopes rose. After all, Maggie was queen of impossible things.

"That doesn't explain why they're worse."

He was right, of course, and I tried again, rubbing my arm where his fingers had dug in. "Maybe we missed something."

"Maybe." His gaze went to Charlotte, three blocks up.

"We can't let her face Maggie by herself," I said. It was true, and anyway I'd have said almost anything to keep from being alone with Curtis right then.

When we turned the corner, Charlotte was already banging on Blooms's door. But the shop was dark like the rest of the street, and the sign in the window read "Closed."

"She's in there," Charlotte panted. "I saw her. She took one look at me and went to the kitchen."

Curtis rattled the door handle, then jogged to an alley and returned toting a rock. "Watch it," he said. Just as he got his arm cocked back, Maggie appeared behind the door.

I held my breath, waiting for another riddle that would fix everything, but she just pointed to the closed sign. "It's after hours," she said, her voice muffled through the glass.

Curtis took a step forward. "Not anymore."

Even her eyes stayed calm. She waved a vague hand over the room. "Oven's off."

I couldn't understand why she was acting like she'd never seen us before, why she wouldn't let us in. For the first time that evening, I stood still so long the chill of the wind bit into me.

Charlotte found her voice before I did, putting her face so close to the door the glass clouded with each word. "We did what you said, moved the river. Nothing changed."

"Except the marks," I called, my voice cracking. "The marks faded. But that . . ."

"That wasn't the deal," Charlotte finished for me.

"You have my congratulations." Maggie nodded. "You are one of the first to get this far."

Like that's all that mattered, finishing some task. "But everyone's still the same," I argued. "Worse, actually."

Maggie didn't shimmer or go translucent, but when she looked me in the eye, the jolt of it was like an electric current. "Yes. I said the remedy would depend on you."

"Ellie tried to move the river without us." Charlotte's voice was shrill. "Is that why it didn't work?"

All the breath left my lungs. This is where they'd turn on me. But if Maggie heard, she didn't give a sign of it. "So, what did you decide?" she said.

Everyone froze. Maggie was staring straight at me, but I had no idea what she meant. "Decide?" I asked, hesitantly.

"About what you found. You did find something?"

"Yes," I said. "We found—you know, but . . ."

"But you didn't think beyond that?"

Sudden joy rushed through me. The task hadn't failed. We just weren't done. Everyone at the hospital was still within reach, but I seemed to be the only one who'd realized that. Curtis was still poised for window-smashing and Charlotte only stood there, her breath cloud growing on the door.

"So, what do we do now?" I said, loud enough to get through to everyone.

Maggie was already drifting, not in body but in mind, staring at something over our heads. "If moving the river didn't show you," she said, "I certainly can't."

When Maggie had vanished back into the depths of Blooms, Curtis set the rock down.

"She means the bones," I informed them. "What to do with the bones."

Charlotte whirled around. "I think we got that, thanks." Beneath the streetlights, the shadows under her eyes were deep as bruises.

"So then you know what we have to do," I simply said. "Tell people what we found and set the story straight."

Charlotte drew herself up, radiating perfection. "And what story is that, exactly, Ellie?"

For a second, the words stuck in my throat. But I couldn't back down, couldn't run away, not anymore. "We tell them we found Benjamin Caster."

Charlotte pointed to the NO CASTERS signs fluttering from the windows. "Don't you get it? Right now, one wrong look could set things off. What do you think a skeleton's going to do? No one will agree on who that is."

"So, they'll run a DNA test."

As soon as the words left my mouth, I knew all the reasons that wouldn't work. Charlotte said them anyway. "And by the time the results come back, we won't have a town left. Anyway, that'll only prove someone died. Not how."

"Harsh," Curtis said, kicking at the rock. "Really harsh."

But Charlotte was right. Bishop's Gap would tear itself up long before I could prove anything, which meant I had no idea what to do now. And from the look of the two of them, standing tense on the sidewalk, neither did they. I swayed on my feet, drained all at once.

A car swung around the corner, the same one as before.

"We should move," Curtis noted and led us past the padlocked office supply store into the elementary school playground. All around the school, houses were dark, like they'd already been abandoned. And soon they probably would be, once the people in the hospital died. Once the shooting started.

Curtis lowered himself into a swing, humming under his breath *when the bough breaks, the cradle will fall* . . .

Charlotte glared at him. "Get up, idiot. I've been thinking. There's just one choice. We have to go to the river and put the bones back under. That might save what's left of the town."

The look he gave her, full of poison and adoration, made me catch my breath. But there was no way we could do what she'd just said, and I dug my feet into the playground mulch, reaching for solid ground. "That doesn't make any sense. Maggie wouldn't have sent us to find the bones just to put them back."

Her eyes narrowed. "Okay, then you figure it out."

But I couldn't, not with the two of them staring at me while above our heads, the moon ticked itself away.

Curtis started swinging, pumping back and forth until the frame shook. I was about to explode from the squeaking when he dragged a foot in the mulch. "Please, teacher," he said, raising a hand. "May I think now?"

Charlotte didn't answer, which he must have taken as permission. "See, what I want to know is—Maggie said we're one of the first. Did you notice that? *One* of the first. So, not first."

Charlotte and I gazed at him. Somewhere in the direction of the hospital, a siren whooped and then died away.

He zigzagged a toe through the mulch. "Does that mean someone's tried this before? And that's why we could still find the old bed? I don't know, it just seems like something we should find out."

He was right, though it took me a second to grasp the full implications of the nightmare. If we weren't the first to have this task, that meant another strand of history ran through Bishop's Gap, a history none of us knew anything about. People before us trying to set things right. Trying—and failing. And all the time, those white bones were reaching up out of the river for us.

I couldn't stop shivering, and this time it had nothing to do with the bite of the wind. Charlotte leaned against the swing set poles, her eyes fixed on the school where the crescent moon reflected from every window.

"Or not," Curtis went on, circling around, twisting the swing chain up. "Whatever you want."

I stopped mid-breath. If Charlotte didn't agree, there'd be nothing left to try. We'd split apart with one day left.

"You're right," she finally said. "We have to know what has been tried before." Her eyes met mine, and there was something in them I couldn't read. If it had been anyone but Charlotte, I would have gone for sadness.

"So, what do we do?" I asked. "Start knocking on doors?"

Charlotte opened her mouth. Then she closed it again. She

looked like she was about to be sick, but in the faint moonlight it was hard to tell.

Curtis unfolded himself from the swing. "Oh, great, that'll work. Ding-dong. Hey, you ever try to move the river in the middle of Oakbend? Two tries, tops, we get locked up."

"So, Ellie." Charlotte looked at me. "Who do you think might know?"

She'd wiped the sick look off her face, but still, I couldn't read her eyes, only the intensity behind them. She knew something I didn't, something I wouldn't want to find out. I ignored my throat closing, the spinning metal playground, and made myself breathe. *For Jean.* This was all for her, wherever it led.

So far, only one person had been a step ahead of me this whole time. Answering questions before I asked them. Understanding about the woods. Unfazed when I showed up at dawn in someone else's clothes, like she'd been expecting all of it. "I know who to ask." My words were loud in the ashy air. "But I have to go alone."

19

AUNT RUBY OPENED HER FRONT
door with its faded mark, eyes tired. "So, are you here for the
night or just a change of clothes?"

"I'm so sorry to keep you up this late," I apologized. "But
could we talk a minute?"

"That a question or a statement?"

I shrugged. "Maybe both."

"If it's about a boy, I don't want to hear it," she said, gesturing
me into the foyer. "I'm too old to be responsible."

I shook my head. "It's not that." And probably never would
be, not with how I'd treated Drew, but I couldn't think about
that now. I took a breath. "Aunt Ruby, I need to know about
the river."

"Well, close the door behind you," she said, pulling a black
dragon-print robe tighter around her bony frame. When she
turned, red crimped hair swung halfway down her back. "Go
on and make yourself comfortable in the parlor," she said over
her shoulder. "I'll be there in a moment. Dinner's long gone, but
I'll rustle something up."

"I'm not really hungry, thanks."

She waved me off. "I never discuss nature on an empty stomach."

In her parlor, plants packed the room, wrapping tendrils up the furniture like the place was a greenhouse. Ivy seemed to grow around a marble-top coffee table right before my eyes, but that was just a trick of the stained-glass chandelier whirling color all around the room. In this place, I could almost believe the woods were a bad dream and Charlotte and Curtis were some faded memory. But then the parrot clock on the wall squawked ten o'clock. If we had until the moon didn't rise tomorrow night, that gave us less than twenty-four hours.

"Aunt Ruby?" I called.

"Just coming," she replied, sweeping in with a tray that held a tall silver teapot and from the sound of it, about a thousand spoons. Banquo panted in next to her, his stump of a tail wagging. Aunt Ruby placed three dog biscuits on a china plate and set it on the floor for him.

"Macaroon?" she asked, holding a pair of silver tongs suspended in midair.

I'd probably need that rush of sugar. "Yes, please." She placed three yellow cookies on another china plate.

"Tea?"

I shook my head. Between the plate and the bones lying in the old riverbed, I already had more than enough to juggle.

"It's plum blossom. Dried it myself."

I couldn't keep saying no, not with Aunt Gert's empty chair visible in the corner of my eye. "Yes, okay. Thanks."

She poured a cup and set it rattling on my plate.

"So, Aunt Ruby—"

My great-aunt put up a hand. "Not before tea, please."

"The thing is, I don't have much time," I told her. "That's why I'm bothering you so late."

She took a sip from a fragile teacup that had obviously shattered at some point and been put back together with Super Glue. "From what I've gathered, you want me to help you. And I'm not sure how to do that just yet." Her blue eyes snapped, young in her wrinkled face. "So, you'll just have to wait a spell."

"Yes, ma'am," I said meekly.

The parrot wings flapped 10:15. I downed my tea in one gulp to get it over with, plum and spice scalding my throat all the way down, only to watch Aunt Ruby drink three cups at a snail's pace. Each time I fidgeted, trying to urge her along, she lifted a hand.

Banquo snuffled the crumbs around my feet, then scrambled up next to me, propping his head on my lap like this was all normal, just another night with everyone safe at home. Sudden tears pricked at my eyes and I swallowed them down.

Finally, Aunt Ruby set her teacup on the marble-top table. "You said you needed to ask me about the river. I assume you don't mean the mighty Mississippi?"

"No, the—the Oakbend."

"Well, what about it?"

I was at a blind bend in the road. If I told her everything, that might break the deal with Maggie, and after trying to move the river by myself, I wasn't about to go down that path again. "I was just wondering what you might know."

She shot me a sharp look over her bite of macaroon. "I know I skipped thirty-five stones over it one afternoon because my brother told me I couldn't. That's your Grandaddy. Always telling people not to do things."

Her eyes were intent on mine.

"*Grandad* used to go down to the river?"

"Laws, yes. We snuck in regular. He dunked us all in that water a time or two, till we got smart. Then we banded together and fought back."

"He never took me."

"No, he wouldn't have. Got to where he couldn't stand the place."

Chills raised the hair at the back of my neck. Grandad couldn't be part of this nightmare. *Please, not Grandad.*

"Did he—did he tell you why?"

"No, never did. I'm not sure it was something he could quite explain."

And there went any help Aunt Ruby could give. So I was stuck in her parlor, holding a plate of cookies with nowhere else to turn.

Then she breathed in deep. "He did his best to tell me, you understand, but I think he didn't know what happened. Not really. Which is why I can't hand over an answer like the solution to an algebra problem. And I don't guess an equation would satisfy whatever's at work here, anyway."

The world stopped, quiet except the ringing in my ears. But I had to know. "So, what did happen?"

"Child, he never got the words out. All I can tell you is that one morning he came home from the forest soaked to the bone. After that, he was different. And he stayed that way."

The clock ticked until I breathed in time with it, too fast in and too fast out. My Grandad—tomato plants, checkers, and all—he was part of the strand that ran through Bishop's Gap. Part of trying to help and failing. That's what he'd been telling me in that checkers game an eternity ago. And I couldn't ask him what he had tried in the past. I couldn't ask him, because of what I'd done.

Aunt Ruby broke into my thoughts. "So that's what I *don't* know. Now I'll give you what I can." She stood, whisked her famous red shawl from the back of her chair and wrapped it around her shoulders. I thought maybe she was headed to the attic for a magic talisman or something. She seemed like the kind of person who would deal in those, and right now, I'd take anything I could get.

Instead, she struck a pose. Banquo grunted and settled further in, pinning me in place.

"The quality of mercy is not strained . . ." Her voice filled the room. It should have been funny, Aunt Ruby reciting Shakespeare in a dragon robe and pink bedroom slippers. But it wasn't.

"It droppeth as the gentle rain from heaven . . ."

She did the whole speech from *The Merchant of Venice*, all the way to *"deeds of mercy."* Then her performing voice died away. "Not a lot of mercy to go around here, is there? Seems like, if years of hatred haven't helped, maybe we should try another way."

She was either crazy or brilliant. But she hadn't been helpful, and she must have seen that on my face, because her expression softened and she bent over, smelling of mothballs and blossoms, to pat my shoulder. "I'm sorry that's all I can offer you, Ellie. For the rest, you'll have to talk to your father."

At first, I didn't understand what she meant. "Wait—Dad?"

She nodded.

"He told you about the river?"

"Didn't have to. Once you've seen it in a person—the haunting—you recognize the signs."

The haunting. That sounded about right, and the strand tightened around my neck. Grandad. Then Dad. Now me.

Aunt Ruby took the plate from my hands. "You won't get the

whole story, Ellie, because he doesn't know it either. But I think you'll get enough."

———————

Aunt Ruby drove me to the hospital in her mint green Buick. She insisted. "It's not safe for you to be wandering the streets this time of the evening, especially now, though I must admit my night vision's not the best. Just yell if I hit something."

We rattled along at ten miles an hour until I wanted nothing more than to scream and never stop. Everything I thought I knew about Dad and Grandad was slipping away, changing the familiar buildings on familiar streets to places I'd never seen before. I clutched at my seatbelt like it could keep me from going under, telling myself that Aunt Ruby was only guessing. She was mistaken, had to be. In a few minutes, I'd have solid ground under my feet again.

But when we finally made it to the hospital and I walked up to Jean's room, I waited about an eternity before going in, trying to swallow down my stomach. Whatever this conversation with Dad turned out to be, it would break what was left of our bond. We could never go back.

Then the veined faces behind all the closed doors called *hurry,* and I knocked instead of going straight in. When the door opened, for a second, I thought Grandad was standing there. But it was Dad who faced me, suddenly old. "Ellie," he said, bewildered, rubbing his unshaven face. "What are you doing out this late?" He frowned. "It's too big a risk, you know that."

"Aunt Ruby drove me." I kept my voice hushed. "I have to talk to you about the task. The river in the woods."

His face contorted, and the last scrap of hope I had that this was all a mistake vanished. He motioned me into the bathroom, and I tiptoed past Mom, asleep in a hospital chair. I didn't dare look over at Jean.

Dad eased the bathroom door closed behind us. Then he turned, close in the small-tiled room. "So, you've heard the rumor. It's a fraud, Ellie. Some kind of sick joke. Just ignore it, okay?"

"It's not a joke. It's not." My voice came out strained, like someone else's, talking to a person I barely knew. "Because I have the task too."

Dad staggered like I'd hit him. "It can't be. It's just—not possible."

My words came out in a rush. "I know. That's what I thought when Maggie first told us, but it's working, it really is. We moved the river, and the marks on the doors—they're fading. I just need to know what to do next."

His jaw tightened. "And who is this Maggie?"

I'd forgotten he didn't know. "She's—she runs a coffee shop. It opened a few days ago in the old five and dime."

Dad picked up a comb at the edge of the sink, then set it down again, distracted. "Look, I don't know why the marks are fading. Maybe that's just what they do when so many come at one time."

Before I could protest, he went on. "Listen to me now. I met a woman at that place too. Pearl, her name was. We did the task—everything she asked." He shook his head. "Even with Lester Finch three sheets to the wind the whole time."

My stomach twisted. Lester Finch had been Curtis's father.

"And we found what was under the river." His eyes shot a question at me.

I nodded. "We found it, too."

He sighed. "I wish you hadn't had to see that. When we did, Finch just collapsed. We thought he'd passed out, so we went into town to tell her. She wasn't there, and by the time we got back, he'd covered everything over again. And, as you've seen so very clearly, nothing changed."

Dad had said *we*. *We* went into town, *we* came back. I suspected I knew the answer, but I asked anyway. "Who else was there?"

A muscle worked in his jaw. For a long moment, he didn't answer. "Daniel Levy," he finally said.

Daniel Levy was Charlotte's dad.

So, Aunt Ruby was right. It was no accident that the three of us had walked into Maggie's café yesterday morning—which seemed a lot longer than a day ago. Our fathers had been given the same chance. And our grandparents before them, maybe all the way back to the beginning of Bishop's Gap. And not one of them had stopped the nightmare.

"Dad, what were you going to do about . . . what's under the river? You know, if Curtis's dad hadn't messed everything up?"

He looked at me. "Forget about that, okay? Just forget it. I've spent my whole life—well, that doesn't matter now." He reached for the bathroom doorknob. "I'm going over to that coffee shop and taking care of this."

I caught his arm. "You can't! Please. And anyway, she's closed for the night."

He paused a moment, then rubbed the stubble on his chin. We were standing on cracking ice now, but I pressed on. "Dad, please. What were you going to try?"

Anger flashed across his eyes and his fists clenched, and for a second, I faced a stranger. Then he forced a smile, relaxed his hands. "Well, if there was any justice in the world, we'd have told everyone. But Levy flat refused, and then threatened to have me arrested. Afterward, I thought . . ."

He stared unseeing at the shower drain.

"What? You thought what?"

"Just what I told you. What I believe to this day. That it was only a joke. That woman laughing up her sleeve at us."

"I really don't think Maggie—"

He shook his head. "Not the person you mentioned. The woman who had the place before, when it was the five and dime. I thought this was all over when she left. It should have been. But one thing's certain. Whatever's going on here, it's not something you need to worry about. First thing in the morning, I'm calling the sheriff in on this."

"I understand now. Really." I kept my voice calm, trying to forget that look on his face. "So, you don't have to make that call. It'll just stir everyone up, and right now, I don't think the town would survive that. We should wait till—till everyone's better." I reached past him to crack the door. "A day or two won't make much difference."

Dad glanced in Jean's direction. "When she's better."

I nodded. "When she's better, I'll tell the sheriff everything. I promise." I stepped out into the silent room, my sister so still on the bed. "I'd better go," I whispered. "Aunt Ruby's waiting for me outside."

"Good. That's the safest place for you right now." He put a hand on my shoulder. "Ellie, sick joke or not, that place dredges things up."

I told him I'd see him later and left before he could tell me not to go back.

20

I KEPT MY HEAD DOWN THROUGH
the halls of the hospital, dodging nurse shoes, IV stand wheels,
and the occasional blur of CDC white. At the exit sign, I made
a break for it, emerging out under a chilly sky where clouds sat
frozen across the last of the old moon. Three parking spaces
down, Aunt Ruby idled with the driver's light on, probably
reading Shakespeare again or something equally unhelpful. In
that light, her profile was like parchment, stark and beaky and
extremely old. She didn't look up, and I couldn't face her, not
with what Dad had just said. I wanted to run straight out of this
nightmare town and never look back. If Dad and Grandad had
failed, odds were, we would too.

Behind Aunt Ruby's Buick, the exhaust plume grew. She'd
wait all night if she had to, run her engine out of gas, her car out
of heat while I ran past the county line, past the state line, out to
anywhere people had never heard of Bishop's Gap or a Burning
Tree. But I couldn't do that to her. Or Jean. Or any of them,
Caster or Levy. Not with a night and a day still left.

When I got into the passenger seat, Aunt Ruby didn't ask
what Dad had said. In fact, she didn't say a word all the way
back to her house while I just sat there, buckled into the worn

leather seat, watching a red glass hummingbird swing from her rearview mirror and racking my brain for any idea about what we should do with Benjamin Caster's bones. When we sailed into the carport, she reached over and patted my hand. "I'll take you to your room."

My room turned out to be the one at the very top of her house, a tower room that smelled like a cedar closet and had a bed so tall I'd have to get a running start to jump into it. Even by the dim light of a hurricane lamp, the bedspread made my eyes ache—stripes and paisleys and polka dots all fighting each other.

The bag I'd brought with me the day before sat unopened in a corner of the room under vine-patterned wallpaper. And those vines were swaying in the shadows, or the shadows were weaving around them. Either way it made my head spin. I grabbed my toothbrush and headed into the tiny bathroom next door, where I washed up in a strange sink with brass clawed feet.

A face ghosted from the shadows when I walked back into my room, and I swallowed a scream. But it was only Aunt Ruby, pulling something from under the bed. "I'd forgotten the stairs for this. Been donkey's years since anyone slept here. But the sheets are clean, you can rest sure of that. I washed them yesterday."

She pushed a small-hinged step stool to the bed, climbed it, and perched on the edge.

I really wanted nothing more than to be by myself to think things out. But Aunt Ruby was clearly settling in, swinging her legs from the side of the bed. "Like I said, I've never been one for confidences, and I don't intend to force one. But"—she patted the spread beside her—"if you need to tell me something, I'm here."

I could see there was nothing to do but climb up next to her and wait this out. She sat there, bony and over-rouged, running her hand along the chaotic patchwork. "All my father's ties," she said, laughing a little. "Mother saved them for decades, stitched them together when he died. Seemed to bring her some comfort."

So, when she did leave the room, I'd be lying under some kind of relic quilt.

"He never could tie them," Aunt Ruby went on. "Got the worst-looking knots you ever saw. Always had to call Mother in to help him."

"Uh-huh," I said, waiting for her to run out of words. I gave an inward sigh. Maybe it would come to me in a dream, what to do with those bones. There really wasn't any other hope left.

"And do you know, one day my mother went out of town—I can't remember where—and I caught him one morning, tying this striped one here neat as everything." She chuckled. "I never told his secret, either. Not till this very moment."

"Dad can't tie his either," I said. "At least, I don't think he can." Though, after all, what did I really know about him? The ache that had been gnawing at me for days turned to tears again, and I blinked them away.

Aunt Ruby was staring straight at the wall now, at the twining shadows.

"Did you get to talk with him tonight? Your daddy?"

I nodded. "Not that it helped."

"Well, there's different kinds of helping."

"This wasn't one of them. I still don't know . . ." I hesitated. "I mean, what to do next."

"Heavens, I hope to goodness you weren't going there looking for what to do. Didn't you hear me say he didn't know?"

"Well, what was the point, then?"

I basically flung those words at her, but she only took my chin in her hand and turned my face toward hers. "You already know,

Ellie. You've known since the second you decided to get back in my car. Let it in, child."

Nails skittered down the hall and Banquo skidded into the room, coming to a stop at the stepstool. Aunt Ruby slid down and picked him up, sat him next to me on the bed, and shook a finger at him. "Now, don't you dare shed all over history."

At the door, she turned. "Ellie. Let it in."

As soon as she walked out, I saw it. The moment I'd been pushing away. The one I hadn't expected. That look on my dad's face, rage and something else, the look that turned him into a stranger. I'd seen that exact expression on Charlotte's face enough times to think it belonged only to the Levys.

But then, I'd hated her back. Hated Drew for choosing her instead of me. And I'd been secretly angry with Jean for being the favorite and generally sparkling through life when all I seemed to do was drag myself along.

Something in the air. It wasn't spores. It wasn't even Burning Tree ash. More than anything, hate filled the air of Bishop's Gap. And I was breathing it out as much as anyone.

I pushed Banquo over and crawled in under mothball-smelling blankets, not even caring that I was still wearing clothes that reeked of the woods. Because now I knew why I'd messed up every single thing I'd tried. I'd been stuck in my own head, so sure I was right just because I was a Caster that I couldn't see anything else, myself least of all.

And now I was done. Out of excuses. Out of ideas. Out of time.

I'd barely turned off the lamp when a tap came at the window, and I looked up to the last person I wanted to see.

Curtis Finch's face hovered on the other side.

21

I PULLED THE BLANKETS UP TO MY neck, gesturing Curtis away, but he was fiddling with the lock and before I could even get the lamp switched back on, he had the window open. My heart skipped a beat. Aunt Ruby was at least two flights down, and I'd never outrun him.

"Get out," I said, hoping my voice wouldn't give away the hammering in my chest. If he came after me, the lamp wouldn't be enough to stop him. "Get out or I'll scream. I'm not alone in here."

"Shhh," he said, pointing a dim hand toward the tree by the window. "Rapunzel's coming. Or are you Rapunzel? Doesn't matter. Only that was one steep tower."

I got the lamp on just as Charlotte appeared at the open window, her face smudged but every strand of hair still in place. I never thought I'd be so glad to see a Levy.

"A little space, Curtis?" she said, getting one hand over the sill.

"Magic word?"

She glared at him. "Now."

"Hey, it's not like this was my idea." Instead of moving, he reached a long arm down and pulled her through the window.

She scrambled over the sill, banging her knee and thumping to the floor as her citrusy perfume floated into the room.

I couldn't face either of them, not now. "Look, you can't be here," I said, as she got up. "Aunt Ruby's right below us."

"Nope," said Curtis. "Other side of the house. And her light went out." He dragged himself away from Charlotte and leaped onto the foot of the bed, landing on Banquo, who nipped him.

His words finally registered. "You've been watching the house?"

"For hours," Charlotte said. She held her arms tight against herself like she was trying to keep this Caster room from contaminating her. "Seeing as how you tend to skip out on people. And you did it again, didn't you, Ellie? Ran over here, left with your aunt, then came back and snuggled up in bed like we weren't waiting."

I nearly slammed back with *Don't let the window hit you on the way out*, but I felt Dad's brand of rage twisting my face and I bit the words off. They would only destroy whatever chance we had left. "That's not how it happened."

"Hey, do you have another pillow?" asked Curtis, propping three embroidered ones under his greasy hair. "This doesn't seem like enough." The throttling look had gone from his eyes, but under the joking, he was tense. Watchful.

"So where did you go and what did you find out?" Charlotte demanded.

I didn't want to tell either of them any of it, but so far, going it alone had gotten me nowhere. I took a deep breath and launched off the cliff. "Aunt Ruby took me down to the hospital—"

Charlotte was on that like a spider to a flea. "To see your dad."

I stared at her. "How did you know?"

"I heard the story a long time ago, about how he went into

the woods with my dad. And how it didn't end well. I just didn't know why they'd gone." She gave a little shrug. "Tonight Maggie told us."

So that's what her expression had meant back there in the schoolyard. All this time, Charlotte Levy of all people had known more about Dad than I did. The ground seemed to waver, and I leaned against the bedpost until it held me steady.

"So, yes, I went to see him," I said in the stranger's voice again. "But he didn't tell me what to do. He said the whole thing was a joke."

She slid down the wall to the floor, her face sheet-white in the moon-flecked room, but she hadn't fainted. More like she couldn't take being vertical another second. "Okay," she said to herself. "And I can't ask Dad because he's . . ."

She didn't have to say anything more. He was in the hospital. And that was my fault too.

Curtis whistled. "Sorry, princess."

"Stop *calling* me that."

"You got it, sweet—"

"Shut up, Curtis." She put a tremulous hand up to her shadowed face, and for the first time in years, she seemed real.

I sank down beside her. "There is one thing," I said. "Not that it helps, really. I found out we can't just put the bones back under the river."

Charlotte looked up, her face blotchy. "That's what they tried?"

I nodded.

"Then what are we supposed to do?"

Curtis sat up, his muscles tight. "I guess we go with Ellie's idea. Tell everyone."

I shook my head. No way could we let the old story loose with a skeleton thrown in and a mark on every door. "Charlotte was right. That would wreck what's left of Bishop's Gap."

"Thanks," she murmured.

Curtis shrugged, but he didn't relax. "That's our two options," he said.

"So, they're going to die," said Charlotte. "All those people." Her voice rose to a pitch that would wake Aunt Ruby blocks away. "We can't—" Her voice almost broke. "I hate her. That Maggie, I hate her." She mimicked the woman's calm voice. "Just move a river. Figure something from thin air. Oh, and—by the way—we're out of coffee."

She'd nailed Maggie, I had to give her that.

"Hey," Curtis said, reaching down and touching her sleeve. "We have time."

"Actually, we don't," I said. And I told them all about the World Tree and the runes and what Maggie had said about the moon.

Charlotte's eyes grew larger and larger. "What do we do, Ellie?"

"I don't know," I said helplessly.

Downstairs, the parrot clock chimed one. Lamplight glinted on Curtis's hair and for a second he was just a red-headed boy, the one who lived a few blocks from Charlotte, always putting gum in someone's hair or lobbing a ball through a window back when Charlotte and I still played tea party with her blue-and-white china, serving each other slices of mud pie with daisy icing, hiding squirt guns under our plates in case Curtis got too close. And for that second, I wanted to help them almost as much as I wanted to wake Jean up.

Charlotte rose to her feet. "I'll go through my dad's desk, see if anything might, I don't know, stand out."

"Want me to come?" I said before I remembered she wouldn't let me anywhere near her house.

She shook her head, but she didn't hit me with the glare I had expected. "You wouldn't know what to look for. But—thanks."

Curtis stood up too. "Well, I'm off to get some beauty sleep."

Charlotte shot him a look. "Are you serious? Everyone's dying and that's your plan?"

"Hey, I'm only a Finch. This has nothing to do with me." There was an edge to his voice, and I saw him double again. The boy he'd been. His scabbed face now. "I'm helping you from the goodness of my heart."

"The stalker in you, you mean," she snorted.

He stiffened, and Charlotte now turned to me. "Ellie, you're not going to disappear again, right?"

Her question was justified, I had to admit that. I shook my head. "I'm staying with this till it's all finished."

"With us."

I held up my oath-taking hand. "With you."

She gave me the smallest of smiles. "Good."

After they both disappeared down the tree, I fell into bed again, stuck under the weight of the covers and Banquo and everything else. A faded yellow mural of the man in the moon at the top of the curved ceiling smiled down on me like some kind of joke. Because Charlotte wouldn't find anything no matter where she looked. Her dad hadn't known what to do any more than mine had.

I saw Jean's face that last night before the mark, every freckle alive. *"What rhymes with muffin, Ellie?"* There was still a chance to tell her. One more day to solve everything. If we could only figure out how.

22

A MOURNING DOVE CALLED, LOW
in the gray dawn. I'd pinned my last hope on sleep showing me
the way, conjuring up the path forward that would bring Jean
back, bring everyone back. Instead, I got bones fusing themselves
together under the river as sirens wailed in my dreams again and
again. It was more exhausting than staying awake would have
been. Tonight at sundown, when no moon rose, Jean would be
gone. She'd slip away with *You really just don't matter that much*
still hanging between us.

In the growing light, the man in the moon winked at me.
Or maybe it was at Banquo, who was lying on his back now,
paws kicking in his sleep. *Hey, diddle, diddle . . . The little dog
laughed . . . And the dish ran away with the spoon . . .*

The dish and the spoon.

I sat up in bed, kicking the blankets off. Charlotte's dad and
mine were dead ends, but there was something left to try. One
more chance to figure this out.

I smoothed the crazy-patterned coverlet the best I could
without waking Banquo and blew a kiss to the painted moon.
Then I tiptoed down the stairs and into the kitchen, propped a
note about going to school early against the aloe plant by the sink

where Aunt Ruby would see it, and eased out to a gray morning. All the faded marks on the doors waited for us to break the town's spell. Proof that we still could.

Last night, Maggie had assumed we'd know what to do, like the bones we'd found made it obvious. But she couldn't see the future, couldn't anticipate we'd still be stuck. So, I had to talk to her without Curtis aiming a rock in her direction and convince her to explain.

I was down the front steps when a patrol car turned the corner. I ducked behind Aunt Ruby's porch railing. The car pulled by slow, and I didn't let out my breath until it was out of sight, though most likely the deputy wasn't looking for anything in particular. There was probably a usual dawn patrol. But then, a block south, two patrol cars idled on a side street, their lights whirling. That made for nearly half the Bishop's Gap force in this Caster neighborhood. I took off without looking back. Whatever had happened, I needed to reach Maggie.

Nearing the malt shop, I understood. A spray-painted message dripped red next to the *LEVYS ONLY* sign, and my stomach dropped.

WE'RE COMING

I knew exactly what that meant. Casters priming their rifles. The deputies would try to arrest the instigators, but that would only delay the shooting, not stop it. And, sooner or later, law enforcement themselves would join in, which was just one more reason I had to hurry.

Only when I got to Main Street, I couldn't find Blooms. I circled the block twice to make sure I hadn't skipped over it. Then I pinched myself. But it wasn't a mistake, and it wasn't a dream. Maggie's shop was gone. An empty storefront stood in its place with no furniture, no light fixtures, not a trace of the letters she must have scraped off the window after we left the night before.

The overcast sky rushed down, seeming to whirl the street around me, and for a second, I couldn't breathe. Maggie must have given up on us or else this really had all been a horrible trick. Either way, I had to find her. And there was only one other place to look.

I stumbled on a ragged sidewalk crack as I turned away from Blooms, which seemed pretty fitting, seeing as how I was about to trust-fall into someone who really might not care enough to catch me.

Curtis came to the door with his hair sticking up over one ear and a wrinkle mark creasing the side of his face. He hadn't been kidding about going home to sleep.

"You have to help me break into the library," I blurted out. There was no point in working up to something like that. He'd either help or he wouldn't.

And he didn't shut the door in my face. Instead, he pulled me into a room where strips of light from broken blinds fell on a jumble of dirty plates piled on the couch and heaps of clothes and empty cereal boxes all over the floor. The place smelled like the bottom of a laundry hamper.

He picked a gray hoodie off the floor and pulled it over his head. "You are the biggest nerd, you know that?"

"I'm not going for the books, Curtis. I need to get in

there because—" I looked around nervously. "Could we go somewhere . . . more private?" I'd never imagined saying those words to him, and I didn't like the taste of them in my mouth now.

He motioned to the dark back rooms. "Help yourself."

"But isn't—" It struck me. "You're the only one here?"

He looked at me. "Who else would there be?"

It was a good point. I should have realized before. Curtis's mom had died before his dad took off, which only left the uncle with dirty nails, the one who cruised by the high school most afternoons at dismissal, staring at the girls coming out. The mark on their door must have taken him, and for once I wasn't sorry.

"Right. Okay. We'll just talk here." I looked around for an empty place to sit. There wasn't one, so I stayed standing in the one clean island of the room. "Maggie's gone. Like, disappeared gone. Her shop's empty too."

Curtis mumbled something under his breath.

"She must have left us some kind of clue. And she knows I go to the library. The first time we talked, she told me I'd been looking in the wrong section, remember? So we have to get in there." I didn't tell him I had no idea where to start searching once we did.

His eyes narrowed. "Even if that made sense—and it doesn't—what makes you think I'd know how to do that? Get you in?"

"Well, for one, last night at Aunt Ruby's house. Two, the water tower. Three, the office supply. Four, Pete's." I sighed. "I'm not stupid, Curtis."

The corner of his mouth twitched. "So, even if I was part of all that, and I'm not saying I was, those were all, you know, dead of night. You're talking middle-of-the-morning Main Street. And that building has an alarm."

"She keeps the code at her house. And a spare key." At least that's where she'd gone the meltingly hot afternoon last summer when she'd locked herself out of the library with her purse and the code inside.

Curtis scratched till his red hair pointed in all directions. "So now you want to B and E a residence."

"Or we could go to the hospital," I suggested. "Try to grab her keys there, turn off the alarm somehow."

He shook his head. "There'd be way too many people wondering why we're not in school. Especially now."

Of course he was right. And I didn't want to step through those doors again with the sickness deepening. Or risk running into Dad.

"So, it's the house, then? Please, Curtis. There's nothing else left to try."

He handed me a pen and a credit card bill with "Final Notice" stamped in red. "Write it down."

"What?"

"Write down what you're asking me to do. So whatever happens, we're in it together. You got that?"

I nodded, scribbled what he wanted. I would have written anything, really, because with ten hours left, I finally wasn't stuck anymore.

He tapped the paper. "Sign it."

"You want a fingerprint in blood too?"

He shook his head, grinning. "We'll burn this when we're done."

23

AT MISS PROW'S HOUSE, TREES spread gnarled branches over the roof, and holly spindled up past the wraparound porch. That was all in our favor, plenty of places to hide, and I hadn't seen a single patrol on the way here. But cars filled the neighboring driveways, and anyone could be watching out of a window. We hurried through an open gate to her shadowy backyard, where the paramedics hadn't even bothered to close the screen door to the porch when they left.

Curtis stopped so fast I almost ran into his backpack. "You sure she's not here?" he whispered.

I nodded. She lived alone, and she hadn't been at the library for days.

When we climbed the rickety porch stairs, the warped floor groaned under our weight. *Go back*, it said, but I couldn't. I'd crossed the point of no return days ago when I set the first match to the Tree. Besides, Miss Prow would give me permission for this if she could. At least, I thought she would.

Curtis tried the back doorknob, then leaned his weight against it. "Bolted." He tried again. "Two places."

There was only one window in the back, and it didn't budge

when Curtis tugged at the sash. "Painted shut. I'll have to break the glass."

I shook my head. "They'll come looking."

"Who's going to come?"

I jerked my head toward the neighbors. Even if they didn't hear the smash, I couldn't let Miss Prow come home from the hospital to a broken house.

Curtis shrugged the backpack off, pulled out a putty knife and a mallet from the front pocket, and wedged the knife under the sill. "Fine. I'll try this first."

When he'd worked the seal free, he stuck the blade right in the center. "Yep, that's a swing lock." He was levering it open when a door slammed at the neighbor's. We hit the porch floor.

Splinters dug into my face while someone yelled that the trash cans wouldn't put themselves out. When the rant stretched on, Curtis muttered something under his breath, slid a hand up the porch wall, and started working blind. By the time the voice died away, he had the window unlocked.

He tossed the tools back in his pack, opened the sash with a crack, hoisted himself up, and shimmied over. Then he grabbed me by the arm and dragged me in after him. As soon as my feet hit the library floor, I pushed away, hoping like crazy he hadn't sensed my heart pounding. And it wasn't just nerves because I'd never broken in anywhere before. It was the room he'd pulled me into. Gray-papered. Dim. The lace-patterned morning light only reached through the curtains far enough to show a plastic-covered sofa. And the air was cold and sour and so heavy with dust, it seemed to be shoving me back. I'd officially stepped over the dividing line to Miss Prow's private world.

Curtis bent to stare at my face. He yanked off his glove, licked a finger, and before I could jerk away, slid it across my forehead. "You got a little blood from the porch there."

"Hey," I said. "Hands to yourself." My arm was still sore from where he'd grabbed it the day before, and the two of us alone in this silent house had me off balance.

He grinned. "We can't have you bleeding all over the carpet, that's all."

He pulled his glove back on, picked up a pair of ancient binoculars from a side table and tossed them hand to hand, like all this was his. My heart raced to overdrive. Miss Prow might have opened her door to me, but she never would have let him in. So whatever he did here, it would be my fault.

I grabbed the rattling binoculars and set them in their dust-shaped spot.

"Just the code and the key, got it?"

Curtis was wandering the room now, touching every single thing. "Right. Where exactly did you say they were?"

"I didn't. I only know one day she locked herself out and came over here for them."

Curtis headed for the door. "That key'll be in the kitchen, under a vase or something."

"And you know that how?"

He smirked at me. "I had a meemaw."

Artificial light fell into the hall from the kitchen, left over from when they'd taken Miss Prow to the hospital. Still, Curtis held up his hand as he crept around the corner, then waved me in to where the sour smell was ten times stronger. In the center of the room, a tiny wooden table held a china cup where a tea bag had dissolved into moldy liquid. Next to it, on a china plate, a biscuit was smeared with brown, cracked jam.

Exhibit A of the night I'd burned the Tree. And beside it

sat a newspaper and scissors. Miss Prow was always clipping something for the thousands of files in the Archives room. "You never know what someone might need," she'd say.

Now that phrase rang in my mind. *What someone might need.* If Maggie had left a clue, it would be there—somewhere in those files. Now I just had to get to them.

I started in on the cabinets to the left of the sink, lifting a thousand blue glasses, teacups, identical spice jars with neat copperplate labels. The gloves Curtis had loaned made me clumsy, and more than once I almost dominoed a row of stemware. Miss Prow must have inherited a whole family tree's worth of breakables she couldn't use.

Curtis was working the cabinets on the other side, and from all the muttering and clanking, he wasn't having any better luck. But we had to find that key soon. Because between the scattered noises, and the breaths we took in and out, a listening pressed around us. Perhaps someone had seen us on the porch after all. Maybe they were right around the corner, waiting.

In a blur of almost-panic, I pulled a chair to check above the fridge and found vases, cut glass, china, pottery in every shade. But no key. And Curtis had already closed the last drawer.

"So, did your meemaw have a backup plan?" I tried to keep my voice light, but it came out shaky and too loud.

He sighed, rubbed his nose with his dirty glove. "Yeah. Hundreds of 'em. Closets, jewelry boxes, you name it."

I ignored the sound the quiet was making. "We'll just have to work our way through." Though that could take years. We didn't even have a day.

"You want to split up? You cover this floor, and I take the second?"

I shook my head. Even with the clock running out, I wasn't

about to trust him alone in this house. Without another word, Curtis started out and I followed him into another chilly hall, this one with a light on in a room by the staircase at the end.

It seemed like the paramedics could have turned off a bulb or two when they took her away, saved her some electricity at least. Curtis stepped over to the door with his fists braced, all show. There couldn't be anyone else here.

That's when it hit me. Miss Prow lived alone. So how had she gotten help? At the doorway, Curtis suddenly bent double, hands on his knees, like someone'd just socked him in the stomach. "Trust me." He straightened to block my view. "You don't want to—go in there. She was up on a ladder when . . . it happened."

I didn't need to go in. I saw her with all her calm certainty, falling in her pleated skirt and her sensible shoes.

"Is she—is she gone?"

"I don't know. Give me a sec." He stepped in, closing the wooden door behind him.

Please was all I could think in the silence as she died a thousand times in my mind, and a thousand times it was my fault. Someone was dead because of me. Not in limbo. Dead. My mouth tasted of ash, like the Burning Tree had finally made its way inside.

The door creaked open, and Curtis stuck his head out. "She's bruised pretty good. But it looks like she's still breathing."

For a second, he was an angel in a sweat-stained hoodie.

"We have to call someone," I said, trying not to sound frantic. "We have to get her help." Or he had to. I was shaking so bad from the relief I couldn't take a step.

Curtis didn't budge. "Okay, and what if they come before we find what we came for?"

"But Curtis—she's . . ." I couldn't put my thoughts together, couldn't hide the shaking, had to grab the wall to stay upright.

"Hey, now." Curtis got an arm around my shoulder, bracing me. "She's been in there, what, three days? And she's still ticking." His voice came steady through the chaos in my head. "So, you want to finish this thing or not?"

"I don't know. I don't . . ."

"Listen, Ellie. If we can fix things, it helps her too. Getting caught won't do her any favors."

He was right. And between that and his body heat, I'd almost stopped trembling. I shrugged off his arm. He didn't seem to notice, just talked on. "Plus, if she's here, her purse has got to be. Wasn't in there, so . . ."

"Bedroom," we said together.

We took the stairs up two at a time. In a room with faded rose wallpaper, a black leather purse sat on a white, four-poster bed. I ran to it and rooted through about a million loose tissues, trying not to think about Miss Prow, how she'd been downstairs, alone, for two nights and three days. Everyone must have been too busy with their own losses to remember her. Or they'd just thought someone else would have found her. The lump in my throat was swelling toward panic again when my fingers brushed a ring of keys.

"Got it," I said, holding a skeleton key marked "Library" up to an empty room.

A muffled bump came from the closet, and then Curtis strolled out with a robin's egg sweater tucked under his arm, waving a piece of paper. "Lockbox was open. Kind of defeats the purpose, but whatever."

"She just didn't have a chance to lock it," I said. "And you're not taking her sweater."

"I wasn't planning to." He led the way back down the stairs, then stopped at the door where Miss Prow had fallen. "Stay here." Moments later, he returned without the sweater, avoiding my eyes. "It's, you know, it's colder in there."

As if on cue, the doorbell rang. "Julia?" someone called. "You in there? Thought I saw you up in your room." Two more rings of the bell. "I've never been more glad. I thought you were down at the hospital."

A face peered through the window on the door, and Curtis pushed me down to the musty carpet.

"*Julia!*"

A few seconds later, whoever it was hammered at the back door.

We scrambled up, and Curtis grabbed my hand. "Did you close the window?"

"I can't remember."

He pulled me toward the front door, and in the rush, I forgot not to look. Miss Prow lay slumped on a wooden ladder in a room full of books, the blue sweater tied around her shoulders. Her face was toward the door, so covered with angry veins I wouldn't have known her. And her eyes were open.

24

I NEVER KNEW I COULD RUN THAT fast, but Curtis still had me by the hand and between his death grip and what I'd seen propelling me forward, my toes barely touched the ground. We didn't stop till we were out of the neighborhood, not until Curtis pulled me into the weeds behind the abandoned Esso station at the edge of downtown. I gasped scorched air, fighting the burn in my lungs.

Curtis sniffed at his hoodie. "Do I smell like that place? Old lady is real hard to get out."

But he couldn't fool me. That sweater he'd given to Miss Prow showed who he really was. "We have to call," I said as soon as I could speak. "Get her help."

Curtis jerked his thumb back in the direction of her house. "That woman'll do it." He handed me the paper with the four-digit code. "And you've got the keys, so—I'm out." He stuffed his gloves into his backpack and hitched it on.

But I wasn't about to do this last part alone. Not when I was so close to figuring out how to help Jean. Especially not with that image of Miss Prow burned into my mind, those open eyes staring at me for hours while I sat alone in her library. Just having him there would take the edge off, but before I could ask, he hissed, "Get down."

A second later I heard it, the lunge and sputter of old engines. A line of pickups wound down the road, carrying Casters from up in the hills, rifles over their knees, exactly what I'd been dreading since those signs first went up in the Levy windows. No deputy could stop this. And Sam Caster was with them, sitting in the bed of the last pickup. Sam, who'd been in my class until the mark hit his house.

"Yep, they're coming for the others," Curtis whispered. "Took them long enough, didn't it?"

I stared at him through the tangled grass. "What do you mean, *others*?"

He raised his eyebrows. "You haven't heard? The sheriff's been rounding Casters up."

"Sheriff *Caster*?"

It wasn't possible. He'd never turn on his own, but Curtis was nodding. "For property damage."

"The sheriff's arresting people over graffiti?"

Curtis looked at me like I'd crawled out from under a log. "More like for trying to burn Levy Sports Supply down."

So those sirens hadn't just been in my dreams. And soon the real violence would start, because burning the sports supply had been strategic. That place carried more than fishing rods and hiking boots for the elite of Bishop's Gap. It was the main source of Levy ammunition.

When the last of the pickups had disappeared into gray air, Curtis helped me up. "You still heading to the library?"

"I have to," I said, my ears straining for shots. We'd hear them any minute now, and the taste of copper filled my mouth.

"Guess I'd better come too." Curtis bent to tighten a loose

bootlace. "But I never did this, okay? Never helped you, never set foot in that place. You got that?"

I could have hugged him. "Got it."

From the Esso station, we took back alleys up to Main. I kept Miss Prow's ring of porcupine keys pressed silent in my pocket until we crouched at the back corner of the library. Now we had to walk up the marble steps and break in during school hours with deputies out and pickups circling. "If anybody asks, we have a research paper due," I whispered. "The history of our town."

"Research paper?" Curtis rolled his eyes, then saluted. "Fine. After you, forest freak."

The street was empty, and we got up the steps okay, but then I couldn't make the skeleton key work. It went in, turned, and nothing. We were so close. If we could just get through this door, we'd unlock the archives, find the right file, and—

"Hey there." The last thing we needed, a voice behind us. We turned to Ralph Finch from the bakery next door, wiping floury hands on his apron. "Can I help you kids with something?" He glanced at the road. "I don't think this is really the best time to be out."

"Yeah," said Curtis. "She left her cool inside." I could have killed him.

"Pardon?"

"Schoolwork," said Curtis. "For a research project?" He shrugged off his backpack, started rooting through it. "I've got the assignment here. They're making us learn the history of Bishop's Gap. Like we don't all know that already."

A look passed between them. Ralph Finch took the piece of paper Curtis was holding out, and I held my breath while he scanned it. Then he nodded, gave it back. "That's an assignment, all right. I got to say, it's nice to see something normal going on. But you two best hurry."

I went back to jiggling the key. Even in the chilly shadows of the doorway, I was starting to break a sweat.

"So, I guess you're planning to stay open today?" Curtis asked, his voice even.

"Yeah. You know how it is. We pretty much get left alone."

Deep in the mechanism, the key caught. With a click, the lock slid back.

"Now, you call me soon as you need a ride," Ralph said. "Don't walk it, okay?"

"Thanks, Mr. Finch," I called over my shoulder. "We'll do that."

"Alrighty, then. And be sure to lock that door behind you."

We stepped inside to the steady beep of the alarm. Curtis tapped in the code as the library wrapped itself around us, old and faded like Miss Prow's house, except with the faint vanilla smell of books. Or maybe that was from the years of bakery air drifting in. A few shafts of light came through the back window, dimmed by dust motes, hundreds of them, suspended.

"We'll start with the Archives room," I said. "Everything about Bishop's Gap is there. If Maggie left us a clue, that's where we'll find it."

The Archives room held wall-to-wall olive file cabinets, a wooden table, and two white bucket chairs. A box with white gloves and a magnifying glass sat on the table. "Fantastic," Curtis said, falling into one of the chairs. "I'm not going to come out of here the same person. I'll end up with glasses, a bowtie, the works."

I shut the door and flipped the lock. That way, if Ralph Finch had second thoughts during bread-rising time and peered in the back window—if anyone did, all they'd see was an empty room.

"You start with A," I said. "I'll work my way through B."

He groaned and pushed himself to his feet. "What are we looking for, exactly?"

"Anything to do with Maggie or her shop. The opening of Blooms, maybe?"

Generations of pack-rat librarians had saved random newspaper clippings, brochures, bulletins, really any scrap of paper that crossed their desk. But nothing surfaced under "Ba-Bl" for Blooms or even "F" for five and dime, just car wrecks and graduations and concerts.

I couldn't stop thinking about Miss Prow caught on her ladder, about her open eyes. Maybe underneath the veins, she knew what was happening. Maybe all the people in comas did—sensed it, heard it. So, if this last effort didn't work, and with every file that didn't help I was more worried it wouldn't, I'd get to Jean's room before the sun went down, tell her the rhyme, tell her I'd miss her, everything. And it wouldn't matter who heard.

The words on the next file blurred through the tears I couldn't blink away.

"Hey," Curtis said, straightening up from a bottom file drawer. "You think I got something here?" He held out an article, dated the year we started kindergarten. It had been filed under "A" for "A New Establishment."

I took it, wiping my eyes, and my body tingled. The clipping showed the grand opening of the five and dime. From what I could tell in grainy black and white, the place hadn't changed since then, and neither had Maggie. So Dad *had* met Maggie. He'd come face-to-face with Memory. Only then she'd had a different name.

"What will you offer this town we don't already have?" the reporter had asked her. Such a ridiculous question since Bishop's Gap had next to nothing. But maybe her answer could solve it all.

"A little bit of everything," she'd said. "What-you-will."

What-you-will. The same words that had been on Blooms's door.

Curtis had seen them too. He underlined them with his fingers. "You think that's a code or something?"

"I don't know. It might be." At least it was a start, proof there could be breadcrumbs here. "We'll just keep looking."

I plowed through two more file drawers in a flurry of searching until a picture of Maggie's shop flashed out again. This time, the storefront was empty like I'd always known it to be, at least before this week. The actual story was about a break-in at the office supply store a few doors down, and I poked Curtis, who was leafing through about a hundred folders, his feet up on the table. "Do you see anything in that?"

He scanned it, then shook his head, but his eyes were laughing. He'd obviously done the breaking in, and I let myself smile back. "Me neither." And I have no idea why, but I kept on going. "You know, there's more you could do with—your skills."

All the air left the room, which seemed to be shrinking around us. I expected him to come after me, but he didn't even look up, just sent another file sprawling to the floor. "Besides looting our fine town, you mean?"

"Well, yes. Something like that." I picked up the files he'd scattered and dropped them back into place.

He kept his eyes on the manila folder in front of him. "You think I'm not planning on that? Think I'm some loser like everyone else does?"

"No, it's—I was *hoping* . . ."

"Now, you, on the other hand, you're showing a real talent for crossing the line." His voice had lightened.

"Be quiet, Curtis."

He smiled. Not a wolf grin, an actual smile, and for a second, at that particular angle, it could have been Drew sitting there. The same jawline, same crinkle at the eyes. Maybe I'd never see that expression on Drew's face again. Suddenly, I had to know for sure.

"Hey, about Drew—does he talk about me?"

Curtis shrugged. "From time to time, I guess. I mostly don't listen."

"Oh."

He looked up, but I couldn't meet his gaze. "Why?" he said.

"No, no reason." What was I thinking, asking him that? I flipped through "Shakespeare Festival. Shelter, Animal. Shelter, Bomb" like my life depended on them.

"C'mon. Why?" he persisted.

"I—with this whole thing—I think I hurt him, that's all." My face burned. I'd just given Curtis ammunition for decades.

But he only said, "Hey, I'll put in a good word, okay? See if I can pry him off Charlotte. Do us both a favor."

I was sliding out the next file, my face still on fire, when he went dead silent.

"Ellie. What about this one?"

He was sitting straighter than I'd ever seen him, and he wouldn't let go of the paper.

When I saw it, I didn't blame him. The picture was of Maggie again at some kind of picnic, which wouldn't have been surprising except the date was sixty years ago. Grandad stood in the background, movie-star young.

I grabbed the magnifying glass and dragged the other chair next to Curtis.

"That's her," he said. "That's Maggie. Right?"

She had different hair, and she wore an A-line dress with pumps. But the circle of magnified dots showed the same face. Calm, unwrinkled. The same gaze. Same exact way of standing. Of course. That was Memory looking back.

"Yes," I breathed, "that's her."

She must have reinvented herself over and over again, always offering the other path. The way out. If there really was a way out.

Curtis scanned the article. "Okay, so, this was some kind of social. They had potato salad, blah, blah, blah, everyone wore something stupid . . ."

"Here it is," I pointed. "*Marguerite*, pictured left, had this comment to offer, 'It's good to see the town come together like this. Perhaps now you'll bury your dead.'"

I sat back, my heart slamming against my chest. There it was. The obvious answer. Bury your dead. So Curtis, Charlotte, and I, the three of us together, had to bury the bones. Really bury them, not just cover them with the river. In our panic, none of us had thought of common decency.

"That's kind of heavy," commented Curtis. "For a picnic."

"It's the clue. It's what we're supposed to do. See? We're supposed to bury him."

His eyes darted to her. "But isn't that what Charlotte wanted to do? Put him back under the river?"

"Hiding him and burying him are two completely different things." The whole room was glowing now, even the filing cabinets. And for once, the air felt clear. *I'm coming, Jean. Just one more thing to do first.*

I grabbed the other article about Maggie and stuffed it into

Curtis's backpack. He was still staring at that picture, hunched over now, intent, searching for something in the background. His meemaw, maybe.

"C'mon, Curtis, this is it. Just pack that up. Once we're done, it's yours if you want it."

He didn't move, a shadow in the fluorescent room. Of all the times for him to get pulled under by the past, just when we had the chance to be free of it.

"Okay, well, stuff it under your shirt or something. We have to get to Charlotte."

He looked up then, his wolf smile firmly back in place. "Yeah," he said. "Charlotte."

25

THERE WASN'T A PICKUP IN SIGHT
as we headed to the school, or a patrol car either. And there still
hadn't been shots, like time was stretching out for us, though I
had no idea why. But when we reached the front entrance, two
deputies stood at the door, a Levy and a Caster, hands on their
holsters, scanning the street. I swallowed. Next to me, Curtis let
his arm go slack. His backpack thumped into the bushes by the
school sign.

"Stop right there," the Levy deputy called, walking down the
steps toward us. "What's going on here?"

"We're sorry about this," Curtis said. "See, her alarm didn't
go off, and she was my wake-up call."

It could work. Curtis always looked like he'd just rolled out
of bed, and crawling through windows at Miss Prow's house had
probably done the same for me.

"Empty your pockets, please."

Mine held the pine needles Drew had given me an eternity
ago, dry and shriveled now. Curtis's held a matchbox and a
crumpled receipt.

"Neither of you brought a backpack?" the deputy asked,
confiscating the matchbox.

We shook our heads. Mine was still at Aunt Ruby's.

He looked us up and down, eyes narrowed. I held my breath. We were so close now, and the minutes were slipping by. "Okay, then. But you pull this trick tomorrow and we're going to have a different conversation, you understand? You can't be out here wandering the streets."

"Yes, sir," I said, and we escaped inside.

We'd come right at lunch period, which was perfect for getting to Charlotte. The cafeteria held its usual comforting square-pizza smell and yellow trays covered the fork-scarred rollaway tables like always, but everything else in there was the twilight zone. Too many empty spaces at the tables. Nobody eating.

We got a few side-eye glances, though mostly everyone was too worn out for any more surprises. Charlotte and Drew sat together at an otherwise empty table. They weren't talking, but even halfway across the room, the air hummed around them, shimmered like bright thread weaving them together, shutting out the world. His head was bent toward her, his arm tight around her shoulders.

Next to me, Curtis tensed, and I knew exactly how he felt. For a second, in the library, I'd thought Curtis's good word might put things right, send us back to the time when Drew never glanced her direction, when he traipsed in the woods with me every afternoon. Maybe Curtis had started to believe he'd have a chance with Charlotte too. But this kind of enchantment wouldn't be reversed. Anyone could see that.

Drew looked up then, not my Drew anymore. A wall stood between us, as invisible and real as the threads binding him to Charlotte. But her expression was pure relief, and I half-ran to their table, mouthing *We found it.*

Drew stood up, blocking my way in the same plaid shirt he'd

worn when we went into the woods for Jean's ceremony, the day he'd tried to comfort me. "I know where you're headed," he said. "And she's not going with you."

Charlotte walked around him, flawless as always. "It's okay," she said. "We'll be back soon."

Drew turned to her, his jaw set. "I can't lose anyone else." He should have been saying that to me. That he couldn't lose me. That he'd do anything.

Charlotte brushed her fingertips down the line of his cheekbone. "Hey, it's going to be okay. Trust me."

"Touching," Curtis remarked. "Really."

It took the edge off the moment, but nothing could make the clock strike midnight, turn Charlotte back into someone ordinary, wipe that look off Drew's face.

"Can't you shut your mouth, Curtis?" Charlotte snapped. "For one single second? Everywhere I turn, you're there." Then she froze, her eyes fixed on someone behind us.

"What exactly is going on here? Please, be precise." Vice Principal Levy stood behind us, her voice flat as always. She'd come up so fast, the tag of her teabag still fluttered from her cup. Above her tweed cardigan, her eyes glittered. "I will not tolerate disturbances of this kind, particularly now, when calm is needed most." The woman turned her gray gaze to us. "Curtis Finch. Your unexcused absence crossed my desk this morning. Strike twelve. I'll see you in my office next period."

And there it was, our straight shot melting away. Not even Charlotte had leverage with this woman, and her wobbly plastic smile wasn't about to change that. We'd have to sit through the rest of the school day with the answer burning through Curtis's dirty shirt.

Charlotte turned to Drew, her eyes pleading. He took a deep

breath. "Ms. Levy? This is about Charlotte's dad. He's a lot worse. She needs to be with him."

I shot him a grateful look, but he didn't catch it.

"Then I will get a call, won't I? Proper channels, now more than ever."

I took Drew's lead, playing off him like we'd always done. "See, that's the thing. Her mom can't get through. The lines are jammed. That's why we're here—to take the message."

Her eyes flickered over to me. "*You're* bringing the message, Ellie Caster? For a Levy?"

"Yes, ma'am."

A murmur ran through the cafeteria. People shifted in their seats.

"Hmm," she said.

I plunged on. "See, that's where we've been. With our folks." I turned to Curtis. "He's been with me, you know, helping."

She took a sip of oolong. Then another. "You have a ride?"

"Yes, ma'am. My Aunt Ruby's waiting in the car."

"I'll need to hear from Charlotte's mother—and yours—by school day's end. Understand?"

When we nodded, she turned on her rubber heels and left the room without a sound.

Even in jelly pumps, Charlotte kept up with Curtis's long stride down the empty hall. "Where have you been? I looked everywhere," she hissed.

"We'll show you," I said, trying not to think of the way Drew had gazed after her. "Once we're outside."

"We should go out the side doors," Curtis observed. "Get a different set of deputies."

We rushed through them only to see Sheriff Caster coming up the sidewalk. His eyes locked on mine.

"Ellie. Curtis. And Charlotte Levy. What are you three doing out of school?"

"My dad's worse," Charlotte said. "I have permission to go to the hospital."

"I'm real sorry to hear about that. But I'm sure you know it's not safe to be out walking. I'll escort you over."

Curtis took a step off the sidewalk.

"Just a second, Mr. Finch. I came on purpose to find you, in fact. You and Ellie."

"What about?" asked Curtis.

"92 Titusville Lane ring a bell?"

All the air left my lungs. Miss Prow's address.

"No, sir," he said.

"Yeah? That's not what I hear." The sheriff's eyes found mine again. "We'll discuss it over at the station."

We couldn't outrun him, not all of us, not at this distance, so we followed him to his patrol car and slid in. Curtis kept his gaze out the window and his back to us. For one splendid second, we'd been about to bury the bones, put this thing to rest, wake everyone up. Now we were trapped. No, worse. We were splintering apart, and I had no idea why.

A deputy's voice crackled over the radio. "You there, sir? We, uh, we need to know what to do over here. It's getting kind of loud."

The sheriff leaned forward. "You find anything more on them?"

Silence. Then, "No, sir."

"Let them loose."

"But, sir—"

"You heard me. I won't turn on my own, not when there's no evidence."

That was easy enough to piece together. Sheriff Caster had told his deputy to free everyone they'd just rounded up for burning the sports supply. Maybe that would be enough to make the pickups turn around, at least this time. But the Levys would have his head and his job too, for letting any of us go. So, no more Caster sheriff.

And we were headed straight to the center of it all.

The sheriff let Charlotte out at the hospital, waited for her to walk through the sliding doors, then floored it to the Bishop's Gap sheriff's department, where exhaust still hung in the air from all the pickups heading out.

He escorted us into a sea of beige—walls, carpet, uniforms. In the silent room, desks faced each other, Levys on one side, Casters on the other. Curtis and I walked between them like a spark crackling down a fuse. The sheriff nodded to a Caster deputy, who led Curtis into a side hall.

All the bulbs in the room became spotlights hot on my face as Sheriff Caster opened his office door. "Just step in here with me a minute, Ellie, if you would." Inside, a row of pictures lined his wall. In each frame, the sheriff, smiling, held up a different rainbow trout, hooked and gaping.

"Have a seat."

I sank into a wooden chair. He settled on the other side of his desk, tapping his fingers together.

"You wanting to unburden yourself, there, Ellie?"

I shook my head, keeping my face neutral. At least I hoped I was. That had worked before. "There's nothing to tell." At least not like he meant. I hadn't stolen from Miss Prow.

"Well, it's natural–in times of stress–to act in ways that aren't typical. I've seen that more times than I can tell you. So, let's come to an understanding, you and I. No need to worry your parents, I think."

He paused, watching maybe for a flicker of guilt.

"No, sir," I said, pressing sweaty palms against the frayed threads of my jeans. "They have enough to worry about right now."

He waited for me to say more, and when I didn't, he sighed. "We'll have to dispense with the pleasantries, I'm afraid. And, all things considered, I'd prefer to put this deal on the back burner right now, except for one thing."

I refused to ask what it was.

He picked up the phone. "Go ahead and send him in."

I braced myself for Curtis rounding the corner, or my dad. But a man from the CDC stepped in. His eyes looked straight through me.

"This here's Bill Burke. Might have seen him around town?"

Burke held up a gloved hand. "Good to meet you, Ellie."

I really didn't want him to know my name. And there was no time for this.

But he launched right into a speech. "Now, we've been trying to put the pieces together on what's happened to your town. Here's what we have so far. I wonder if you can fill in some of the gaps for us." Burke ticked off the facts on gloved fingers. "One. Patient zero lives at your house. Two. Your grandfather called this office about a prowler the same night the tree burned. Three. You've subsequently embarked on a string of, let's call it . . . aberrant behavior."

He perched on the edge of the desk, way too close. I nearly choked on the disinfectant smell.

"Now, everyone I talk to says you're the one to ask about the woods. We'd like to know, specifically, about that tree. Anything unusual about it the night it burned?"

I tried to swallow again. "I wouldn't know. I used to go for walks around there, that's all."

The sheriff learned forward. "Ellie, you're in some trouble here. Best tell him. You want to help us out, don't you? You'll be helping yourself too."

The only way I could help was getting out of here, only they'd never believe that.

I spread my hands. "I wish I could. I just don't know."

"Okay, then." Something had changed in the sheriff's face, disappointment, maybe. Or triumph. He reached under the desk and set a clear bag in front of me. My red sneakers were inside, and even through the plastic, the burn marks showed clear.

26

THOSE SCARRED SHOES, THEY TOLD the whole story, and everybody in the room had read it. On the other side of the desk, Sheriff Caster folded his arms. Next to me, Bill Burke leaned back, looking sure I'd cave.

It was only five steps to the door, but then there'd be a line of deputies to stop me. And even if I made it through them, I wouldn't be any better off, not with Curtis still stuck here. We had to bury the bones together, and with Charlotte, or it wouldn't work.

I pictured Jean scribbling in her pink poetry notebook, pictured the marks wiped off all the doors. For courage. For a steady voice. Then I took a breath and told as close to the truth as I could. "Yes, that happened at a bonfire. The wind blew some sparks. I got lucky, stamped them all out. They're my favorite shoes, so I kept them."

The sheriff didn't move a muscle except to say, "We got Curtis in the other room with the same question. Think he'll back you up on that?"

Would he back me up? I'd told him bonfire too, though there's no way he believed it. "Of course he will," I said, squaring my shoulders. "It's the truth."

The sheriff stood, hitched up his belt. "I'll just step out a minute, if you'll excuse me."

Once he left, a taut silence fell on the office, the kind where a person might blurt out the whole truth without meaning to. On the other side of the door, a phone rang. Someone answered, held a staccato conversation, then lapsed into silence again. Burke studied the fingernails under his clear gloves, turned them back and forth, the light falling like polish on his hair. I couldn't read his expression, and I would have given anything not to be alone with him in this room. The sheriff wasn't exactly on my side at the moment, but he was still a Caster, and the air vibrated with a trap about to spring.

Sure enough, in a second, without looking up, Burke said quietly, "Seems to me, Ellie, you could save us all a lot of trouble if you'd do two simple things."

I didn't ask what they were.

"One, tell us what you saw when you burned down that tree. Could be important, with symptoms on this scale."

"I already told you I didn't have anything to do with that. You should test the ash."

He glanced up, sharp-eyed. "We did. That came back inconclusive."

Of course it did. It always did.

"Which is why your testimony is essential. And two, we need a physical from you. With bloodwork. Three jabs, tops." His expression shifted like he'd tried to smile.

"I'm not sick."

"No, but you and Jean grew up in the same environment. We'd test you to see what anomalies she may carry."

"You mean whether she has *spores* and I don't?"

"That, yes. Or if you're affected differently by them. See,

that could be the key to curing this thing. And we'll need your statement to interpret the results correctly."

His light brown eyes gleamed with the certainty he was right, and I couldn't breathe. I couldn't keep my feet still, either. They were itching to get out of here, back to the river. I wrapped them around the chair. If he knew I wanted to leave, he'd never let me out.

His calm voice droned on. "It's your only choice, really."

"My shoes got burned at a bonfire," I said again. "Curtis will back me up."

Before he spoke, Burke straightened the papers on the sheriff's desk, then separated a tangle of paper clips into a neat line. "You misunderstand me. I don't care if you walk out of here free or not. My only concern is having our best bet at solving this. And that's you, Ellie—having you here, helping us, not wandering around the woods as you've been doing."

My heart skipped a beat. "Wandering the woods?"

He looked up, his eyes boring into mine. "Ah, yes. As a matter of fact, your father has told us the whole Bishop's Gap fairy tale, about the, what was it he called it—the Burning Tree? And the skeleton under the river."

The room spun. Dad wouldn't have told any of that, not to an outsider.

But Burke wasn't finished. "He thinks that's where you were heading today. Is that right?"

Now I understood, and I stared at the office wall, anywhere but into those searching eyes. Dad was trying to protect me, using this man to keep me from going back into the woods.

Burke leaned forward until I could smell the mouthwash on his breath. "That would simply be a waste of time. See, my people are doing forensic analysis on those bones as we speak.

You won't be getting anywhere near them again." He waited a beat to let that sink in. "I'm afraid we simply can't let you pursue a fantasy while your sister loses ground."

I was still trying to comprehend that we wouldn't be able to bury the bones and finish the task, when what he'd said about Jean hit me.

"Is she getting worse?"

"Her appearance certainly indicates it, though her vitals don't. Yet. But they will, and soon. Some diseases progress that way—a plateau and then the cliff."

My Jean, drifting away from me in that horribly white hospital bed. His words took her into some clinical world where I couldn't follow. And there was no way to help her now. No way to help the others. Everyone in the hospital would be gone because of me. I didn't even know how many.

I sat rigid in my chair as Sheriff Caster walked through the door. He shot a look at Burke. Burke nodded.

"Seems like you and that Finch boy are pretty tight now," the sheriff said. "Looks like what you said checks out." Then he squatted down so we were eye-to-eye. "But you know as well as I do, it's about to be war here, Ellie. We survived the first move, but they're going to be back. Anything you can give us, we need it."

There was no task left in the woods. So I could do what they wanted, take their tests—which would only show, beyond a shadow of all doubt, that this illness wasn't caused by spores. But maybe in the meantime that would give people some hope, stave off the killing a little longer, and I was opening my mouth to say *Okay, I'll do it,* when a crash came from the other side of the door, then a percussion of chairs scraping back. Calls of "Ma'am? Ma'am!"

The door flew open. Aunt Ruby, her eyes blazing, blew into the sheriff's office like something from another world. Her long shawl sent the trash can spinning across the room, scattering paper shreds across the beige carpet, snapping me back to life.

Charlotte followed in her wake, looking faded for once in comparison. She must have left the hospital and gone straight to get my aunt. Which was exactly the right thing to do.

"Luke Caster. Why in the green world are you holding my great-niece?" Aunt Ruby snatched up the bag that held my shoes. "I saw these, just this morning, in the guest room of my own house. I gave you *tea*, not permission to search the premises."

Bill Burke stood up since the sheriff was obviously at a loss for words. "Ma'am, I can't confirm or deny any of that, but you must see it's an extraordinary time."

Aunt Ruby focused on him, her eyebrows raised. "Of course it is. It always is. And you've just confirmed or denied your way out of usefulness. Leave the room this instant, or I will summon a lawyer to give you enough red tape to hang yourself on."

After a brief moment, Burke did as he was told. I didn't blame him.

Aunt Ruby faced the sheriff, who didn't look anything like his grinning pictures anymore. "Now, Luke, what is this about?"

Sheriff Caster nodded toward Charlotte. "Step outside a second, Miss Levy, would you?"

Charlotte shot me a *stay strong* look. And for a fraction of a second, next to her sequined jeans, her fingers were crossed.

Once the door closed, the sheriff said, "Ellie was seen breaking into Julia Prow's house this morning. With an accomplice."

I froze. Not even Aunt Ruby could talk me out of this.

"Seen by whom?" she said, hands on her hips.

"Now, you know I shouldn't say."

"And you illegally pawed through my property, but perhaps that's also something I could overlook. So now, seen by whom?"

The sheriff sighed like she'd pushed all the air out of him. "Sadie Levy."

"Sadie—Levy?" Aunt Ruby snorted. "We both know she couldn't see a telephone pole if she walked straight into it."

"Now, Ruby, we've got her written statement."

"And I have one for you as well. If you'd be so good as to bring me a pen—fountain, not ballpoint—and a fresh sheet of paper."

Sheriff Caster wavered, deflated. Underneath, he was nothing but exhaustion. "Guess I can let you take her while we double check. As long as she *stays with you.*" He emphasized those last three words.

"And the boy. What's his name? Finch."

The sheriff had already lost, and he knew it, but he didn't go down without kicking. "Now, Ruby, if he didn't do this, he's done something."

She leaned over his desk, red hair flaming. "That is a perversion of justice, and you know it."

The sheriff looked around her at me. "Ellie, we need you to go to the hospital—take the tests. Tell them everything you know. Please. Would you just do that? For the town? For my wife? That's all I'm asking."

Aunt Ruby straightened to look directly at me and take my hand. "Do you agree to that?"

For a second, I wavered. If there was even the slightest chance those tests might turn something up, maybe I should take them. We were probably too late to bury the bones anyway. But maybe we weren't. Maybe the bones were still there. I couldn't leave Curtis and Charlotte dangling off the edge of hope. For this fragile sliver of time, we were together again, the three of us, plus Aunt Ruby. They were the chance I had to take.

27

"NO," I SAID. "NO TESTS."

"There." Aunt Ruby arranged her shawl back around her shoulders. "So let them go."

Sheriff Caster nodded to a deputy, and we stepped out into a silent room where everyone had heard the choice I'd just made. Charlotte raised her eyebrows as Curtis stalked up, sullen and rumpled. But we were together.

"Okay," the sheriff said, rattling the keys in his pocket. "I'll escort you home."

Even if all he did was follow us to Aunt Ruby's place, we didn't have time for that. "Thanks, but that's okay," I said quickly. "My aunt will take us."

She nodded. "My shotgun's in the Buick. We'll be perfectly safe."

The sheriff opened his mouth to argue, but I interrupted. "And I'm sure you're needed here, right? With everything that's going on."

He couldn't say no, not to a roomful of Levy deputies, so he waved a hand and stepped back to let us pass. But by the look he gave me as I walked by, this wasn't over.

Outside, the singed smell of downtown wafted strong, and I

scurried into the passenger's seat of Aunt Ruby's ancient car like all of Bishop's Gap justice was on our heels. Curtis and Charlotte piled into the back. As soon as the doors slammed behind us, Charlotte grabbed my shoulder. "What do we do now?"

"Can you drop us at Grandad's?" I asked Aunt Ruby. I was about to add *and hurry* when she screeched out of the lot so fast, I nearly knocked my head against the window. In the back, Charlotte slid into Curtis and her too-sweet perfume took the edge off the air, but just for a second. "Hands to yourself," she hissed.

"Get off me, then."

It wasn't a fantastic start. I just had to hold us all together a few more minutes, and then we'd know if we could put this right. I dug my fingers into the worn leather seat, every nerve straining toward the moment we'd know we weren't too late.

Aunt Ruby's rings flashed in the dim fall light as she turned past Meet and Three's, still closed. The barbershop. Closed. Hudson's. Closed. All the *LEVYS ONLY* signs, tattered around the edges now.

Charlotte hunched against her side of the seat, clinging to the door handle. "So, what is it? The rest of the task."

I glanced at Aunt Ruby, who was absorbed in swerving around a squirrel that couldn't make up its mind.

"It's okay," said Charlotte. "I already told her about the river." Which didn't matter, not anymore. One way or another, the whole town would know by sunset.

I looked at Curtis, and he fumbled in his pocket and handed the wrinkled clipping over without a word. Charlotte turned her back on him to read it as we flashed through a neighborhood with curtains drawn in all the windows. Here and there, a few people were out on their porches, wearing masks and sitting perfectly still in their rockers.

Charlotte looked up. "I'm not sure about this, Ellie."

"But don't you see? That's Maggie."

"I get *that* part."

A hint of her old tone stung me, and I couldn't keep the edge from my own voice. "She told us what to do, right there. Paragraph three."

"But how is that different from what our dads tried? They put him back under the river, and nothing changed."

Curtis grunted. "Yeah. That's what I said."

I glared at him in the rearview mirror. "That's not what we're going to do. We have to bury him properly."

"Like in a box?" Charlotte seemed confused.

"Like in a grave."

"Burying words," said my great-aunt. "All of you together. That sounds about right."

"You mean ashes to ashes and dust to dust, Aunt Ruby?" said Charlotte.

Aunt Ruby. Like she was family.

"You could use those words, sure. Just so long as it's not *pitch him back where he came from,* I think you'll be fine."

Charlotte let out a breath, settled back against her seat. "Alright. I understand."

The houses were spreading out now, the beginning of fields showing between them, and beyond that, the jagged edge of the woods. My heart revved. Only a few more blocks.

"Oh, yeah, I get it." Something in Curtis's expression made my stomach clench. "So, we're just going to dump some dirt and then you get everything you want, don't you, Charlotte? You, too, Ellie. And no one has to pay."

My brow wrinkled. "I don't understand. Pay for what?"

Aunt Ruby bumped around a gravelly corner at top speed, missing a leaning mailbox by inches. "You got something to say, Mr. Finch, best be out with it now."

Above the beat of the wheels on an unsurfaced road, ashy silence filled the car. Charlotte shifted. She must have dropped her stranglehold on the door handle. "He won't. Never does."

"You're just a shining princess up there, aren't you, way up in your Levy can't-climb-to-me tower." Curtis leered. "It's always been that way, always going to be. I mean, it's right there in that picture. Where are the Finches? Where are they? It's always about Levy and Caster, Caster and Levy, and we're just caught in the crossfire."

I turned in my seat. "That's not—" I started, but Charlotte broke in.

"When we're done with this, you're out of my life," she said. "Out. Got it?" She wasn't putting on the ice queen act now. That was just Charlotte, meaning every word she said.

Curtis saluted, a fake grin frozen on his face. "You got it."

"And do you know why?"

Whatever it is, please don't say it.

"Because once we fix the marks, idiot, you'll be the thing that haunts this town."

The smile dropped from his face.

"She didn't mean it like that," I tried to quickly amend.

Charlotte smoothed her hair behind her ear. The scar on her forehead stood out on her flushed face. "I absolutely did. You've seen the way he looks at me."

Grandad's house was in sight now, and the woods were so close. We couldn't fall apart, not here.

"Well, people change." The words came out as lifeless as

they'd sounded in my head. It should have been more, especially after Miss Prow's house, but at that moment, I couldn't come up with anything better.

Curtis sank into his corner, retreating into himself.

"I couldn't agree more," Aunt Ruby said, studying him in the mirror, a crease between her eyebrows.

I turned to her. "They're going to be there at the river. The CDC. Maybe deputies too. We'll need a distraction."

Aunt Ruby tossed her head back, patting her purse, the worry line easing. "You know if there's anything I excel at, my dear, it's a performance." She turned into Grandad's driveway, muttering, *"As I did stand my watch upon the hill, I looked toward Birnam, and anon methought the wood began to move."*

Only Shakespeare again, but it called up that rot of terror from the night I burned the Tree and the woods seemed to come after me. I shut my eyes, but all I could picture were bare branches, twining to a net.

———

As soon as Aunt Ruby rolled to a stop, the three of us jumped out. She skidded into reverse, heading for the main entrance to the woods as I rushed to the barn, but someone had double padlocked it, and there wasn't time to find another way in for the shovel. We'd have to figure something else out when we got there.

I turned and ran with nothing in my mind but getting to the bones. The others' footsteps thudded behind me, and we'd just made it through the fields, dodging brambles around the honeysuckle corner, when I halted. Curtis skidded so close his hot breath hit my neck.

Drew stood at our old meeting place. This was where we'd always made up after a fight, and my stomach fluttered like a sky's worth of wings. The spell must have broken somehow. He'd come for me after all.

"If I can't stop you, I'm coming with you," he said, and before I could answer, he walked past me to take Charlotte's hands.

"You can't," Charlotte told him. "I'm sorry. That's the deal."

"Then I'll wait. Twenty minutes and I'm coming in."

"An hour," she responded, squinting at the sun low on the horizon. He took her chin in his hand, leaning in to kiss her forehead. The butterflies in my stomach all went wrong, and if everything hadn't already been going in fast forward, I would have thrown up. He was all Charlotte's now.

"Tick tock," said Curtis, staring daggers at them.

I took a deep breath. "Let's go."

28

MY EYES STUNG. EVERY SPLINTERY
breath stabbed. My heart pounded through my ribs, and it wasn't
just because we were so close to the bones. Or because Drew
had kissed Charlotte right in front of me. It wasn't even that
I'd just brought these two into my last hiding place. As soon
as we were inside, the woods folded smothering arms around
us. With each careful step we took, a stench grew like burning
tires, rotting through my core, till I could hardly hold a haze of
thoughts together.

Next to me, Curtis was back to his old cold-sore face, as far
away from me now as if we'd never really talked, as if the library
had never happened. Charlotte had seen to that. And no matter
how fast I ached to get this over with, we had to take the pine
straw path slow so it couldn't sneak a whisper out to whoever
else was in here. Toe, then heel, and repeat. The silence around
us pressed the world away until it seemed there was nothing on
earth but these woods.

Something rustled in the underbrush and Charlotte startled,
her hand momentarily grabbing at the air. Even in the dark
afternoon, she glowed, better than me in every single way. Soon
enough we'd bury Benjamin Caster six feet under, or as near as

we could manage, and then I'd never have to talk to her again. The sun would set just after five, which gave us an hour to bring him to rest, make everyone well.

If he was there. *Please,* I thought. *Please.*

I stepped off the path into a mess of roots, ancient ferns, baby trees grabbing at my legs, and headed toward the river. We weren't more than a few yards in when a hum of voices drifted through the thick air, men's voices. Curtis ducked down, and Charlotte grabbed my arm, mouthing, "What do we do?"

I did the only thing I could think of—dodge trunk-to-trunk until we could see what we were up against. Just as the rush of the river joined the voices, yellow caution tape came out of nowhere, and Curtis jerked me back, pushed me down. An elbow jabbed into my side as my face scraped against dirt-smelling bark, but I could still see into the clearing. Next to the empty riverbed stood a Caster deputy and two people I'd never seen before in full hazmat suits, one with CDC on the back, the other, the forensic analyst.

And white bones lay on the ashy bank. They were there—still there, waiting. For the first time since the mark on our door, something had gone right. Energy pulsed through me. We could fix what I'd done to Bishop's Gap. It was already late afternoon, and we'd have to dig the burying hole with no shovel, but it was all still possible.

The men moved like underwater divers, slow, deliberate, gathering around a camera the analyst held. The pressure lifted on my ribs as Charlotte edged away. A twig snapped under her pink jelly heel. We froze, but they didn't. Just went on, *click, click, click.*

The deputy, holding his hat in front of his nose and mouth, said, "You fixing to pack all this up now?"

The analyst shook his head. "Burke called in an archaeologist. With bones this old, we have to get the okay to move anything."

Just leave. Please. Leave. The sun wasn't going to stand still for this.

Deputy Caster checked his watch, and the analyst, who'd been sliding a lens into its holder, paused. "You got somewhere to be?"

The deputy put his hat back on his head, nearly choked on the air, and covered his face again. "Just wanted to check on my kid, that's all."

"You know why we're waiting. We have to make sure none of this gets disturbed."

The deputy nodded, leaning against a tree.

They were running the daylight out. And the night that was coming would take nearly everyone I loved away. I racked my brain like crazy for some kind of distraction if Aunt Ruby didn't make it in time, but all I could think about was sitting around our breakfast table with Jean, eating pancakes in the shape of tigers.

Next to me, Curtis stared straight ahead, his expression blank. Charlotte's face twisted with panic. Neither of them would be any help, and I was about to come out from behind the tree, no matter what, just from wanting that picture to be true again, when a warbling voice cut through the leaves. *"Who can impress the forest, bid the tree unfix his earthbound root? Rebellious dead, rise never till the wood of Birnam rise."*

Aunt Ruby.

I'd never been so glad to hear anyone in my life. The men whirled around. Charlotte whispered, "Yes!" I might have too, except I wished my aunt had picked something else to recite—that mercy speech she'd made in her parlor, maybe.

"Fear not, till Birnam wood, do Dunsinane, and now a wood comes . . . Arm, Arm, and out!"

I half-expected the trees to go after her, and from the way everyone else was eyeing the woods, I wasn't the only one.

"What in the ever-loving world?" asked the man with the camera, incredulous.

The deputy had his hand on his holster, and even at that distance I could see it shaking. "Yeah, that's Ruby Caster. She's crazy as a speckled loon."

"Fear not, till Birnam wood . . ."

"She's coming this way," he said. "I'll intercept her."

The analyst gestured at the deputy's holster. "You stay here. Stop anyone who tries to set foot over that tape." He pulled off his hood. "You should get yours off too," he said to the man with CDC on his back. "Don't want to scare her the rest of the way out of her wits."

They splashed across the river and out of sight.

Two down. One to go. The deputy spun his hat in his hands, turned to face the bones, then reeled back around, eyeing our patch of the woods. He kept glancing over his shoulder, like he thought those bones might rise up, obviously getting ready to run. My world snapped into sharp-edged focus—the sway of the leaves around me, the dirt under my fingers, Curtis smiling like a scarecrow, though I'd liked it better when his face was stone. Charlotte had tensed, ready to spring.

Hang on, Jean. Just a little longer now.

Aunt Ruby's voice, closer than I'd expected, rang clear through the heavy air. "I'm not feeling so well. Oh, I'm not well at all."

Deputy Caster pulled his gun from the holster as Aunt Ruby's voice rose to a screech. "They're coming! Don't you see them?"

A shiver ran down my spine, though I knew this was just Scene Two for her. Then a thud sounded near where I'd heard her last. Two thuds.

With one final backward glance, the deputy clapped his hat on his head and took off, gun in hand. A few seconds later, I heard him groan. "Oh, now, Ruby, what did you do?"

"Fate felled those men," she said, and the hair pricked up all over my scalp. "The woods are coming for you, too, Andrew Caster."

"Ruby, that ain't sound. You know it ain't sound. And from what I see here, I got no choice but to take you in."

"Whatever you think, Deputy. I'm sure you know best."

"I got to radio this in." A burst of static, then a muffled curse. "Well, anyhow, show me your hands." Cuffs clicked, and then the crunch of their footsteps disappeared into silence.

She'd pulled it off, though I had no idea how. When I started to get up, Curtis put out a hand. "We've got to check it out first," he whispered. "I'll go."

He was gone an eternity. I'd counted two hundred and five seconds by the time he came jogging back, his eyebrows raised. "You take after her, Ellie," he told me, "and you'll be all right."

"What happened?" Charlotte asked.

"Those two guys are just laying there in the mulch. She knocked them out cold with something, I'm not sure what, but it smelled really sweet all around there. They're tied up with that scarf thing she's always wearing."

I could picture her wrapping the shawl around them, her red hair loose and flaming through the heavy air.

Charlotte looked terrified. "They're going to wake up way before we're done."

Curtis smirked. "Doesn't matter if they do. They won't be moving for a while, at least not before the deputy gets back. I made sure of that."

"But they will move again." I studied him. "Right?"

His eyes gave nothing away. "Eventually, yeah."

I shot a glance at Charlotte. She shrugged. "Let's get to it then."

"Now, where's the shovels?" Curtis said.

We wasted time we didn't have finding flat rocks, sticks that wouldn't bend under their weight, and twisting off pieces of vine to lash it all together. By the time we'd finished cobbling shovels together, the light had changed, sending clawed shadows across the clearing.

We had about twenty minutes or so left to dig the six feet. For once, Charlotte helped from the beginning, but under the ash lay hard-packed clay, breaking our makeshift shovels every few strokes. And each time Curtis's hand touched Charlotte's, which was a lot, she jerked back, and he dug half-speed for a while, sulking.

But nothing could break my momentum, not even the bruising shovels. As the ground peeled away in clumps, it seemed I should do more for Benjamin Caster than just bury him under it. But with each thud of dirt, I was erasing the veins on Jean's face. Bringing Grandad back. Freeing Miss Prow.

Once we'd broken enough ground that we could get our arms in up to our elbows, Charlotte sat back on her heels. "I think that's good," she declared. "We don't have a lot of light left."

"Okay, so who gets Mr. Bones?" Curtis said.

I took a deep breath. This was the part I'd dreaded since we started digging. "I'm pretty sure it has to be all of us."

We stood by the fractured skeleton a second, staring down

at the frame that had once held a face, a beating heart. Curtis reached down and grabbed the skull through the eyeholes. "Top down," he said. "Lay him out in order."

It took me three tries to pick anything up, and even for Jean's sake I could hardly bear the smooth rattle of fitting him together again, despite Curtis humming *the foot bone's connected to the ankle bone* the whole time.

In the end, I had to wash the feeling off in the river before I gagged, and I was drying my hands on lichen when Curtis walked over to Charlotte. She was already spading little mounds of dirt over what was left of Benjamin Caster.

"Look," he said, his profile silhouetted by the sinking sun. "I know I've said things—I didn't mean them."

Charlotte ignored him, and he tapped her back.

"Stop it," she hissed.

"You don't want Drew. He's nothing but baseball and flannel."

"Go away."

"Hey, I'm not what you think. Ask Ellie."

Neither of them glanced my direction, which was just as well. I couldn't make words come. Couldn't breathe, couldn't move, couldn't risk making this all fall apart.

Charlotte stood. "I know exactly what you are, thank you very much. You're the roach under my shoe."

The sun was behind their shoulders now, making Curtis seem more than he was. A force. He might as well have been carved from granite.

Charlotte turned, stepped away. "We have to keep going."

I sucked in a lungful of stifling air. We would still finish.

But Curtis didn't move. "You think there's anyone in that nightmare town I care about?" His voice had a dangerous edge. "We're better off without them."

She reached for the shovel, and he grabbed her arm, spun her around. "You. It's always been only you."

And Charlotte did the last thing I'd have ever pictured. She spit full in his face.

The look in his eyes sent me running blind toward them, slashing down everything in my path. This was the last gasp of the Burning Tree, the curse taking hold. We'd all been breathing it in too long.

In one motion, Curtis grabbed a stray rock from the pile and forced Charlotte to her knees. "Stop right there, Ellie." He hadn't taken his eyes off Charlotte. "Time to beg."

29

I STOPPED FIVE STEPS AWAY. IF THE
set of Charlotte's back meant anything, she wasn't about to beg.
And Curtis still had his hand up. There was a nasty edge on the
rock he'd grabbed, like he'd been planning this.

He was bluffing, had to be.

But all around us, flecks of ash were rising, gathering
together, glowing like embers, forming shapes out of the smoky
air, becoming the people from the old portraits. The movie that
had been playing in my mind all my life, about how Jeremiah
Levy had burned down Benjamin Caster's house and then
murdered him, became Simon Finch. He was out of his mind
with fever, his face twisted with jealousy, facing Jeremiah Levy
under a crescent moon.

Near them, Benjamin Caster stood rooted in place, still in
emotional shock from losing his wife and baby. He watched
Simon Finch kill Jeremiah without moving a muscle to stop it,
and when Finch came for him, he ran.

I stood frozen. The Burning Tree had just shown me what
happened all those years ago in this exact spot. Maybe because,
just now, we were reenacting it.

Everything I thought I knew stopped, rewound, and started over.

It wasn't a Levy who'd burned down the Caster house. It was Simon Finch, crazy with fever and more. He'd killed Jeremiah Levy, buried him under the Burning Tree, and changed the course of the river to hide what he'd done. Only it hadn't stayed hidden, that old injury. It seeped into the roots of the Tree, breathed out through its leaves, its scarred trunk, and charged the air with ash and blame. It seared the houses of the families who blamed each other, who'd hated each other enough to start a feud and marked them with calamity.

So, there was nothing between Levy and Caster, no murder, nothing but old stories with the wrong *Once upon a time*. All around me, the world went limp as a puppet when its strings dropped.

"Pretty please," said Curtis, and the edge in his voice was no bluff. "Say it, sweetheart."

"Please," Charlotte finally whispered, but she was too late. The last light had left the trees, the sun slipping under the horizon. There'd be no moon tonight. So there'd be no one at the hospital left to save, Jean gone beyond my reach.

I would have screamed but Curtis's voice cut me off. "You think that's enough? One word?" He twisted Charlotte's arm, forcing her head to the ground, and I had a sudden vision of my world without her. No more doors shut in my face. And Drew would come back.

I certainly couldn't stop Curtis now, out of his mind from the Burning Tree in the middle of the woods. He'd kill me first.

Charlotte moved her head to look up at me. One of her ridiculous shoes had come off, lying sideways, its pink glitter covered by ash. In the dim, I couldn't see her scar, but she was nothing like the laughing-eyed girl at our tea party all those years ago. Or the ice queen.

Curtis grinned his wolf grin. "Time's up."

This was my chance to run, but my feet wouldn't move. I couldn't watch him do this, not the red-haired boy I'd known all my life, not after what he'd done for Miss Prow. Even if he was always this way. And I couldn't stand by and watch Charlotte fall, turn my back like Benjamin Caster and Dad and all the Casters between them. There was no way to save Jean now, or fix Bishop's Gap, but I could get one last thing right. Trade my life for Charlotte's.

I ran through my own shriek into a tangle of arms and legs, to the fury on Curtis's face, his unfocused eyes. I pushed Charlotte out of his reach. He jerked me back by my hair and the stone slammed into my head, an explosion of fierce light. Pain cracked through my skull, and I hit the ashy ground, mouth smothered in the dust.

Curtis's dirty sneakers stilled. Then he lurched away, out of sight. I tried to lift my head. A few feet over, Charlotte lay unmoving. I wanted to crawl to her, but a dizzying stab of pain stopped me. From the pit, Jeremiah Levy's half-buried bones stared up at us. They'd never be laid to rest now.

It didn't matter. Nothing did now the sun had slipped away. Blackness closed in around a stir of ferns at the edge of the clearing. Then, through the nothing that was taking me under, a wisp, a breath.

Clear air.

30

JEAN'S HAZEL EYES BLINKED DOWN at me. Behind her, white curtains blurred into white hospital walls. I could hardly see her for all the light dancing around.

"Ellie?" She was inches from my nose, much too close to yell like that, but I didn't care. The veins had gone from her face. She was just as she'd been, except thinner, maybe. Less bounce.

My Jean. I ached to jump up, wrap my arms around her, but a sick heaviness kept me still. I was scrambling to figure out why when she said, "Can you hear me?"

I nodded. "I'm sorry," I rasped. "Jean, I'm sorry." I tried to prop myself up, but they'd tied me down with tubes, a needle taped into each arm, and each movement split my head down the middle. The haze of the woods rushed back, that feral look on Curtis's face, Charlotte's hair splayed over leaves where I'd pushed her away. And we hadn't buried the bones.

Mom hovered beside Jean, her eyes bright as ferns, the red curls of her hair alive, radiating, though maybe that was just the fluorescent lights. "Baby!" She took my hand, ran her fingers down mine again and again like she'd done when I was little and couldn't sleep. She pulled Jean close, linked us together like a coming home, and then her face crumpled. I'd never seen Mom like that, convulsing, tears running down her face, not even when Jean got sick.

Dad came behind them, unshaven, and no way to tell where the shadows under his eyes ended and he began. But he laid his hands on Mom's shoulders, and when he spoke, his voice sounded right. "Welcome back, Els. Just lay still, sweetheart. You took quite a whack there."

Tears slipped down my cheeks too, and I couldn't put up a hand to stop them.

Mom took her arm from around Jean and pressed a buzzer. A Caster nurse glided in, her face relaxing when she saw me awake.

Mom gently took my hand. "Ellie's back. And I think she needs something for the pain."

If that's why they thought I was crying, I'd let them. I wasn't about to say anything as stupid as *I thought I'd lost this. All of this.* And my head did ache. The nurse raised my bed, sending everything spinning, and gave me something to sip from a straw. Still, the word hurt when I croaked it out. "Grandad?"

"He's resting at home, baby doll," Mom told me. "He's fine."

"He's more than fine," declared Dad. "He's pretty proud of you."

Grandad was home. And Jean was here. Somehow, something we'd done in the woods had worked.

Fear stabbed me. "Curtis?" My voice caught. "And Charlotte?"

Dad pulled up a chair by the foot of my bed and sat down. "Curtis ran away, honey. Nobody knows where."

"So, he didn't go after her—" I couldn't finish.

Dad shook his head. "Drew found both of you pretty soon after it happened and immediately got help. The worst Charlotte Levy suffered was a couple of bruises and a broken shoe."

All I could feel was relief. Curtis hadn't meant to hurt me—the woods had tricked him like they had everyone else. Charlotte was alive. Drew had saved me. And I knew without having to ask that the rifles had been stowed.

Mom still held my hand in her warm grip, and I wanted to ask about Miss Prow and Aunt Ruby too, but I wasn't about to lead them down either of those roads.

"Can we go home?"

"Soon," Mom replied, tucking the sheets in around me. They were already tight, but it didn't matter. "Soon."

The day dimmed with Mom holding my hand and Jean snuggling up against her. Dad stayed in the corner, buried in a newspaper. Right at sunset, a determined hermit thrush sang his lungs out by my window, and I nestled down between the cool, heavy sheets, drifting off with the world put back together.

No, not back together, not exactly. New.

I woke again in the mostly dark to a nurse changing out my IV. Rays of light reached under the blinds and fell on Dad, who'd pretzeled himself between two hospital chairs, snoring up a storm. Mom and Jean must have gone home sometime in the night while I wandered in a half-dream, trying to fit the puzzle of the woods together in my fuzzy brain with the beep of the machines and Dad sawing away a lullaby.

The nurse turned to go.

"Could you open the blinds?" I asked.

"Sure, honey."

They slid apart to a sun rising into a forget-me-not sky. I'd never in my life seen the air so clear. The rush of what we'd done—bringing everyone, and Bishop's Gap, back—swelled my heart. "You need anything else, you just call," the nurse told me. Her name badge read S. Levy, and she was smiling at me. A Levy. The shock of that was almost more than the clear air.

As she walked out, still smiling, Dad stirred, unbent, then came over to place a hand on my forehead. "How are you, Els? Do you need anything?"

"No. I'm okay." I pointed out the window. "It wasn't a hoax, Dad."

"So I see," he replied.

But something was hanging in the air between us, his face still half-stranger, and I plunged ahead. "I don't know why it worked. We were supposed to bury the bones, and we never got the chance. Curtis went after Charlotte and I—I had to stop him."

And just like that, the last piece of the puzzle dropped into place. Benjamin Caster had watched his friend die without lifting a finger to stop it. So a Caster had to save a Levy from a Finch, in that exact spot. That's the wrong we had to right. Trying to bury the bones hadn't been a waste of time. It had gotten us there, together.

"That was the task, Dad."

Tears glistened in his eyes as he brushed hair back from my face. "I'd worked that much out myself. Charlotte told us what you did. We're really proud of you, Ellie. I can't tell you how much. I just wish I could have spared you all of this. That's what I keep asking myself. Why I couldn't." He looked into my eyes. "It was never about not wanting to. I hope you know that."

I tried to swallow past the sudden lump in my throat. "I—I think it was because you didn't see the sweater. Or the buttons. And the tea set, maybe."

His eyebrows rose. "Your head hurting you again?"

I could see why he'd think concussion from what I'd said, and I tried again. "What I mean is, when you went in nothing mattered except he was a Levy and you were a Caster. You didn't see each other, not really. So, I guess the quality of mercy was still strained." That probably wasn't much clearer, but it was the best I could manage. Aunt Ruby would be proud of me.

The tautness went out of Dad's shoulders then, and the corners of his eyes crinkled. "You know who you sound like."

"I know."

"You want to watch that."

The moment still hung fragile between us. I reached for his hand. He held mine tight and regarded me.

"It's still not going to be perfect here. You realize that."

"I know, Dad."

He grinned, color seeping back into his face. "But they took down those *LEVYS ONLY* signs, so I think we can safely say we're headed toward a heck of a lot better."

———————

Just after my mid-morning assessment, Jean's head appeared around the hospital door. "Good," she said, prancing in. "You're awake." I couldn't stop looking at her, and it wasn't just because she'd come back to us. It was as if for the first time, I saw her in full color.

She turned to Dad. "I need a minute *in private.*"

He tried to cover a smile as he folded his paper. "I think I'll stroll down to the cafeteria, see what they have on today."

As soon as he'd gone, Jean pulled out her notebook, and I

tried to get my medicated thoughts together for whatever word she needed help with now.

Instead, she said, "I wrote this for you last night." She stood very straight, for a second not like a kid at all. "Here it is:

I was lost, you came and found me
Pulled me up out of the water
Or whatever held me under
Maybe quicksand
Maybe caves
So I love you more than muffins
I love you more than puffins
I love you more than anything I see.

See, I found the rhyme," she said. "Puffin, muffin."

No words could be enough to follow that, but I said some anyway.

"I like it, Jean. I mean, I really love it."

"Good." She twirled, her hair spinning out like gold.

"And button," I said.

"What?"

"Button kind of rhymes with muffin too. I've been—meaning to tell you."

She stopped twirling with a jerk, pulled a purple gel pen from the spine of her notebook, and held it midair. I knew that look. "I'll do a series," she declared. "The muffin poems."

"You'll be famous."

Jean was already drifting off to a world where only buttons and muffins mattered, but I called her back. When this moment closed, we wouldn't talk again about what happened, I knew.

"Hey, Jean, could you hear us at all? I mean, when you were sick?"

She pursed her lips. "I can't remember. Just that I had to hold onto a string and you were on the other side, pulling me back."

I swallowed hard. "Jean, we all were."

She shook her head vigorously. "No. It was just you." Then she hugged me, and her strawberry-scented hair fell all in my face.

By noon, I was propped up in bed, eating vanilla pudding with a plastic spoon while Mom got lunch down in the cafeteria and Jean scribbled away in the chair next to Dad. When someone knocked on the half-open door, Dad raised his eyebrows at me and I nodded, sending the room reeling. "Come in," Dad called out, and my hands shook so I could hardly hold the spoon. Maybe it was Drew. He was all this day lacked to be perfection.

But instead, Charlotte stepped in, looking like her internal dimmer switch had been turned down a few notches and clutching a huge teddy bear from the hospital gift shop. Part of me didn't want to see her, didn't want to be reminded of the woods that night. And I really didn't want to think about how she and Drew had probably been together all this time, which was why he hadn't come.

Dad tapped Jean on the shoulder and they both went out, leaving us alone. Charlotte clicked across the floor, set the bear on the foot of my bed, and sat in the chair Dad had just left, all without looking at me. She crossed her legs into the perfect pose I could never manage. The room was off balance again, but this time it had nothing to do with my head. It was the emptiness between us. No more Levy versus Caster. Just before the woods—and after.

Then Charlotte looked up, her eyes red from fighting back tears. "I wouldn't have done that for you." Her voice shook. "That's what I keep thinking." She didn't seem to know what to do with her hands, just kept smoothing her hair, fiddling with her purse strap.

"That's okay," I said. Really there didn't seem to be any other answer. And of course it was true. Charlotte couldn't even make room for me at the lunch table.

"So, what I mean to say is—I'm sorry and I hope you can forgive me." She said the last part so fast it came out like one word.

Plain and simple, I didn't want to. Not just because of what she'd admitted, but for all those secrets whispered behind my back, a life's worth of invitations I'd never received.

"I really . . . hope you can," she said finally, looking me in the eye.

The familiar tongue of anger licked at me, calling back the look of rage on Dad's face. Rage—and hate. It churned in my throat, darkened the room around her. But I refused to be another Burning Tree. Drew was right. I had to let it go. All of it.

"I can," I made myself say through the scorch. "Yes, I can."

"Thanks," she whispered.

For the first time since our tea parties all those years ago, we were at peace. And I couldn't go another second without knowing why. "I have to ask you something too."

She gave a small smile. "I can't say no."

"Could you hand me that glass of water?"

She handed it over, confused, and a flush rose in my face. That's not what I'd meant to say.

"Thanks." I set the water down after a decent act of drinking it. "The water wasn't the question, though. Here it is. You're going to tell me what happened. Between us, I mean. Because one day we were shooting Curtis with water pistols and the next you acted like you'd never seen me before." That version of Curtis made me wince, his fiery cowlick hair, the spark in his eyes, and I pushed away dual twinges of fear and curiosity. He'd be okay, wherever he was, now that he was out of Bishop's Gap.

Charlotte didn't answer. The teddy bear with his big red bow that said *Get Well Soon* stared at me blankly. Eventually, she sighed. "The three of us have always been roped together, one way or another, haven't we?" She uncrossed her legs, then crossed them. She sighed again. "My dad found out we were *socially bonded.* I think those were his words." She lifted her hair to show the scar. "It's not easy to forget a thing like that."

For the first time in my life, I felt sorry for Charlotte Levy.

She clasped her hands in her lap. "That's when he told me something that had happened in the woods. He said your Dad had the chance to help the town and didn't. He told me you were the same, and so you were to blame." She lifted a shoulder. "I was six, so—I believed him." Then she grabbed her purse. "I'd better go."

I couldn't let her, not like that, and I blurted out the first thing that came to mind. "So, truce?"

She glanced at me, then nodded. "Yes. Of course. Truce."

"And how's—how's school?"

"Well, everyone's back—it's just the same, I guess." She laughed and I was somewhat surprised how good it felt to hear that. "Except the VP. She keeps stalking the halls, patrolling for people in comas. I think she liked things better that way."

That made me laugh too. Until my head ached again. Charlotte slipped out of the room when the nurse brought me pills in a little paper cup. And when she'd gone, I was alone in the room for the first time, facing the goals scribbled for me on a whiteboard.

1. No INFECTION.
2. MANAGE PAIN.
3. GET UP AND WALKING.

And with that last one—walking—the clench in my stomach came back like it had never left. Soon I'd have to walk out of here, back to the outside world, Charlotte's world. By now, everyone would know I was the one who'd burned down the Tree and kicked off the nightmare. I still had to face Drew. And I could never return to the library.

In that happy fog before Charlotte had walked in, I'd pretended everything was over and done. But it wasn't, not for me. Not yet.

31

THREE DAYS LATER, I WALKED down the empty green-and-white tiled hospital halls, steady on my feet and with only a dull ache at the back of my head. The version of these halls clogged with patients and panicked family and emergency codes had dissolved like a bad dream. Two days after everyone recovered, the CDC left, so Bill Burke was probably still running and rerunning tests with no explanation at all. Nurses waved as I passed them and at the exit doors, Doc Caster gave me a thumbs up. I waved back with my vase of wilting daisies and the card in Drew's scrawl, *Glad to hear you're better.* The only words I'd had from him.

The doors slid open to the crisp air of a late November afternoon and for a few seconds, I couldn't think about anything but breathing it in. Then Dad's truck pulled up. They'd tied pink balloons all over it and someone had written "Welcome back, Ellie" in bubble letters on the windows. Jean jumped out of the passenger side. "We're having hot dogs tonight," she said excitedly, hugging me. "Then a marshmallow roast and then movies. And I'm not even going to tell you about your room."

"Yes, you are," I said, grinning and hugging her back. "You're going to tell me right now."

She shook her head, miming zipping her lips, and Dad came around to help me up. I slid in after Jean, and though she kept on talking, I didn't really hear a word. The marks were gone from the doors we passed. Not faded, gone. And when we turned onto our road and the woods came in view on the other side of the fields, it was only a line of trees—nothing more. No smoke. No haze. No ash.

I was still processing a world with normal woods when we pulled into our drive. Jean wanted me to keep my eyes closed till I saw the room, but Dad said the last thing we needed was for me to fall and break my head again. So, instead, she grabbed me by the hand and dragged me in, past the random knothole where the mark on our door had been.

Mom wasn't in the kitchen, and she wasn't upstairs, and when we came to our bedroom where the velvet squirrel sat on my sister's pink bed, I slowed but Jean pulled me past it. She took me up the attic stairs to the wide room at the top of our house where Mom was sitting, eyes twinkling, in a window seat that hadn't been there before. They'd painted the walls white, and the ceiling sloped down on both sides over a bed—my bed. A yellow lamp sat on a table, and a green rug lay on the white floor.

"You like it?" asked Jean, hugging my arm. "Say you like it."

Mom stood up, her smile glowing. "We thought you might like a quiet place, sweetheart, to just . . . be—especially after . . ." She waved the rest of the sentence away. "But if you'd rather everything stay where it was, we can put it all back."

"Yes," Jean put in. "I even saved the spiderwebs."

"Keep them," I told her. I looked at Mom. "This is—it's perfect." And it was.

Jean was bouncing up and down now. "We can have sleepovers! You'll come to my room, or I'll come to yours . . ."

Mom put her arm around Jean. "Right now, you'll come with me to the kitchen and help me get supper. Ellie, my dear, you rest till we call you."

While Jean skipped down the stairs, Mom drew me in so close I could feel her pulse beating through mine. "You gave her back to us," she whispered. "Our whole lives." Then she took my face in her hands, smiling through her tears, trying to sound stern but failing. "But don't you ever, ever think about doing something like that again, you understand me?"

I nodded, tears in my own eyes. "I won't. I promise." She wouldn't let me go until I did. And anyway, it wasn't a circumstance that was likely to repeat.

When she left, I turned back to my room, stuck somewhere between laughing and crying. The first pink of sunset caught my window, and I pushed it open, letting in fresh air and a hint of pine. It wasn't hard to picture a golden World Tree connecting everything now, the bridge from our woods straight to heaven. But the center of those woods lay empty, and for a second, I felt homesick for something I'd never seen—our Tree before we ruined it.

Below me, Dad lit the barbecue, and a plume of smoke went up. A second later, it vanished. Of course. There was nothing left in Bishop's Gap to leave the mark.

And, standing there at the open window, watching the sun sink into dusk, I realized . . .

I had no idea how to live in a town like this.

32

ON MY FIRST DAY BACK TO regular life, I choked down a glass of orange juice, fresh squeezed from the fruit that had just begun to spot in Dad's patent-pending container. Then I pushed scrambled eggs around on my favorite china plate, the yellow one Mom always set out for special occasions, until the kitchen clock ticked down to no way out. Bishop's Gap High had been bad enough when I was invisible. Now everyone knew my name.

I'd wanted to face everything right away, but Mom kept me home for a week with no visitors, hadn't even let me out to see Aunt Ruby, who was locked up at the sheriff's office for assault by flora—and she had a point. At the hospital, I'd been getting around fine but as soon I settled into the attic room, I could hardly make myself move, like memories weighed down my muscles. Every time I tried to sketch, I saw that look on Curtis's face. Miss Prow slumped over the ladder. Drew turning away from me. Every time I closed my eyes.

And I'd come to a decision. I couldn't help what Drew thought of me now, but I could let him go. Be happy for him, even. When it came right down to it, I'd saved the town, and that was enough. But none of it took the nerves away, the amends I had to make.

"Ready, Ellie?" Dad stood by the door with his keys and a too-wide smile.

"Sure," I said, trying not to throw up.

When he dropped me off at the main entrance, I stepped into a blur of normal. No more papers blowing across ghost-town halls. Backpacks coming at me from all directions. The usual faces. The usual announcements. But in homeroom, everyone stared like I'd just arrived from Pluto—everyone, that is, except Sam Caster who was back in class, smiling at me. Then they started talking about Oakbend, no one bothering to whisper or hide their words behind their hands. I'd expected anger, braced myself for it, but this was worse. A whole new kind of alone.

Right before the late bell, Drew entered, taller than I'd remembered, his blue shirt pulling across his shoulders. He didn't glance in my direction but still my pulse raced. Charlotte came in right on his heels, scanned the room, and gave me a little half-smile before they sat down together at the back.

They sat together at lunch, too, the two of them alone at a table that might as well have been the other side of the world. She waved me over, but this was the wrong place to make peace. For a second, I stood by myself, holding my tray with the chicken-fried mystery meat and cooling mashed potatoes, stuck in the familiar cafeteria wasteland, until Tasha Levy pulled me over to her already full table and found me a chair. Before this moment, Tasha had spoken two words to me, tops, her whole life.

"Did you really burn down that tree?" she breathed as soon as I'd set my tray down. Abbie Finch leaned in. Across the table, Josh Levy raised his eyebrows, waiting.

I had to face the question sometime, and at least by telling these three the whole school would know by the dismissal bell. "I can't confirm or deny."

Tasha flashed a smile around the table. "I knew it."

Now they'd start in on the forest freak part.

"That is so," Abbie began, "what's the word?"

Josh leaned back. "I think you're looking for *epic.*"

And just like that, my world flipped. I belonged at their table. But the tide hadn't just turned for me. All across the cafeteria, Levys and Casters sat together like it had always been this way, like our town had never been split in two.

At their corner table, though, Drew and Charlotte weren't talking, and they weren't gazing into each other's eyes, either. More like they'd run out of things to say. Without meaning to, I caught Drew's eye and he looked away, color rising in his face.

"You have to come with us after school, Ellie," Abbie was saying, interrupting the sudden pounding of my heart. "The caramel apple malt is amazing. Epic."

"Not today," I apologized. "I can't. Sorry."

"Tomorrow, then?"

I nodded as Sam Caster stopped by our table. "You're all coming to the fish fry Saturday, right?" He was looking straight at me. "Four o'clock. My place."

Josh Levy stood up and for a second, my mind shifted, and I thought he was going to shove Sam away. But instead, he only said, "You know it. I'm bringing ice, right?"

I sat back, dizzy from all the doors that had suddenly flung wide open. But I couldn't step into this new life, not yet. There was one more thing I had to do. *The* thing. The one I'd been running from.

I waited fifteen minutes past the detention bell till everyone had left the school and most of the teachers' cars had gone. Then I searched the shrubs for Curtis's backpack. He'd done a good job of tossing it, so it was still there, a hint of blue canvas deep under the holly. I fished out Miss Prow's keys and let the rest be, just in case he ever came back and needed it. Plus, I really didn't want to know what else he had stashed in there. I already knew more than I could take.

The keys weighed heavy in my pocket all the way to Main where the *LEVYS ONLY* signs had been taken down and the graffiti scrubbed away. I burned time peering through the blank windows that had been Blooms, trying to settle the twisting of my insides. It was only one more block to the library, one more block to where everything might unravel. Miss Prow could call the sheriff and slam all the doors shut again. I hesitated. Everything was fine in Bishop's Gap now, better than before. I began turning for home when something moved inside Blooms. A shadow.

"Maggie?" My heart stopped. I wanted to cry on her and thank her and ask her what in the world I should do about Drew. Mostly, I wanted to see her face again, the calm eyes that gave nothing away. When no one answered, I ran around to the back and banged on the door. "Maggie!"

It opened just enough for an arm to reach out and pull me into a faintly coffee-scented room. Then the door slammed shut, a lock clicked, and the reek of Funyuns and woodsmoke closed my throat.

"Don't scream," Curtis whispered. My hand went to the back

of my head before I could stop it, and he relaxed his grip. "Hey, I'm not going to hurt you, Ellie. I promise."

He was thinner than he'd been, paler, eyes hollow. The nightmare of the woods filled the room, and I took a step toward the door. Three more and I'd be out of reach. Curtis didn't make a move to stop me, but something in his eyes held me there.

"Look, I'm sorry." His words echoed off steel ovens, granite counters. In the corner of the room, empty chip bags littered the floor next to the jacket he'd spread out for a bed. "Really. I didn't mean to lose it like that."

I tried to believe him, but I couldn't forget his face that night, the expression I kept trying to sketch away. And he still smelled of the woods. So, I couldn't say what he wanted me to, only, "We all thought you'd run."

His shoulders sagged. "Yeah, I tried that. Got to the county line before I turned back."

If Charlotte knew Curtis was still haunting Bishop's Gap, she'd never be able to sleep through the night. And neither would I.

"You should try again," I said, though right now Curtis at large didn't seem much better.

"I can't, Ellie. Running won't change it—what I did."

He stood there in his stained hoodie, looking me in the eye, miles away from the person who'd forced Charlotte to her knees, made her beg, and slammed me to the ground. More like the little kid I'd known, the person he'd been at Miss Prow's house. "It's okay," I said, the words spilling out in spite of myself. "You didn't know what you were doing. It was—that place."

"You think so?" This time, his voice didn't clear a whisper.

I nodded, and he swallowed hard. "Well, you're right about one thing. I can't stay here, not with you knowing where I am. So you have to come with me."

"Are you crazy? I can't leave Bishop's Gap."

He grinned, a hint of his old self, and pulled the hoodie down over his forehead. "Relax, forest freak. We're not going past downtown."

33

CURTIS PUSHED THE BACK DOOR of Blooms open, squinting in the sunlight. I held my breath for any hint he might turn on me, but he didn't break stride until he stopped at the sheriff's office, where Aunt Ruby's voice drifted out from an open window at the back.

"If we shadows have offended, think but this and all is mended, that you have but slumbered here while these visions did appear . . ."

"We can't go in there," I whispered. The sheriff's office was the last place I needed to be with someone else's keys in my pocket. "You know what they'll do to you?"

He didn't answer, just held the front door open. And I had to step through it. If Curtis was about to tell all he knew, I'd have to explain for both of us.

Inside, most of the deputies were wearing earmuffs to block out Aunt Ruby's voice. They stiffened when they saw us, darted glances at one another. I wanted to run to her, away from this beige room that suddenly didn't have enough air, but Curtis walked right up to Sheriff Caster's office door and knocked. When the sheriff stepped out, his eyebrows went up to his now neatly combed hair. "Well, I'll be. Ellie Caster and Curtis Finch."

"I need to turn myself in," Curtis stated, his face pale around the blotches. "For assault."

Behind us, the room hushed. The sheriff's mouth dropped open. He gestured us into his office, closed the door behind us, and stuffed a towel under it, muffling Aunt Ruby's voice. Then he dropped into his chair, motioning for us to sit.

I tried to keep from trembling and rattling the keys, giving myself away. But the sheriff's eyes stayed fixed on Curtis. "Look, son, I appreciate you coming in. We've been pretty worried, after what happened and all."

"I guess you can go ahead and read me my rights."

The sheriff tapped a pen on his desk. "Well, not so fast. Around here, we're pretty much of the mind that your actions were the woods' doing." He turned to me. "Is that how you see things, Ellie?"

I nodded, not trusting my voice. Curtis would go free, and I'd spend the rest of my life looking over my shoulder. But maybe I'd get the same loophole.

Curtis shook his head. "That's not what—"

"It was that Tree, Finch," Sheriff Caster broke in. "And nobody's pressing charges."

Curtis half-rose as he grabbed onto the sheriff's desk. "It wasn't the Burning Tree, and it wasn't Oakbend Woods. I mean, not all of it."

The sheriff leaned back. In a far room, Aunt Ruby's voice rose and fell, her words indistinct. "Well, then, we're over a barrel," he finally said. "Because I don't believe taking you to court would benefit this town. Or do you much good, either. So, barring that, what exactly would you have me do?"

My stomach wrenched. Curtis was practically begging for

help and Sheriff Caster couldn't see it. I wanted to stand up, demand something, but I had no idea what that might be.

Curtis straightened. "You can send me away. Anywhere but with my uncle," he stipulated. "Somewhere I can clear my head." He sat down then, his shoulders erect for the first time since I'd known him, and I let out my breath. He'd leave, but not running. On the town's terms.

Sheriff Caster studied him for a moment, then nodded. "Sounds like good sense to me. I can arrange that. I'll get things set up now, in fact, if that's what you want."

"Yes, sir, it is."

The sheriff glanced at me. "You can go on then, Ellie. We'll just be working out the details here."

I left before he thought to ask more questions, because the woods hadn't made me burn down the Tree or break into Miss Prow's house any more than it had forced Curtis to pick up that stone. Aunt Ruby was still reciting, and I followed her words like a thread to the end of the hall. She was striding back and forth behind bars, as much at home as she'd ever been, even without her shawl.

She cut off mid-speech. "Well, there you are."

"Hey, Aunt Ruby. I'd have come sooner but . . ."

"But they've been coddling you like an egg," she said, appraising me. "Which I have to say, it looks like you needed."

I managed a smile. "I'm better now. And Curtis turned himself in."

"Well, good for him. That boy's got more going than he lets on."

The keys clanked in my pocket and a flush crept up my face. "So, how long do you have to stay here?"

"Just as long as they'll have me."

"Aunt Ruby, really."

"Oh, a month. I have a commuted sentence, though I want it on record that it's not for good behavior." Her eyes twinkled. "Extenuating circumstances, you know."

I laughed, couldn't help myself. "Oh, yes. Textbook. Does Aunt Gert need anything until you get back?"

"From what I hear, our house is so stuffed with casseroles, you couldn't set a toenail in the place. But thank you for asking."

She cocked her head, and for a second, I thought she was going to burst into Shakespeare again. Then she pointed a ringed finger at me. "Wipe that look off your face, Ellie. Remember, all is mended."

I shrank a little. "Almost all."

"I see," she said. "Then up and at 'em. No niece of mine slinks around this town the way you came down that hall. Especially not you."

"But I don't know how . . ."

"Oh, yes, you do, or you wouldn't be skulking. Go on, now," she said. "Get. And don't come back till you can look me in the eye."

Curtis was nowhere in sight when I flew down the hall, and I'd almost made it through the outside door on Aunt Ruby's swift kick when Sheriff Caster snagged me.

"Wait just a second there, Ellie."

He held out the evidence bag with my burned shoes. I wanted to lace them up on the spot and at the same time, I wanted to throw them away. I wanted this whole thing to disappear. He handed me a yellow form. "I was holding off on this till you'd recovered. But now seems as good a time as any."

"Yes, sir."

"That's community service," he said, pointing to the form.

"Ninety hours, roughly what you cost this town in—let's call it forestry damage. I don't care what you choose to do as long as you get every hour signed."

I couldn't take my eyes off the scorch marks on my shoes.

He cleared his throat. "Also, Curtis wanted me to give you this." He handed me a smudged piece of paper folded over about a hundred times. "And Ellie?"

I looked up. He was holding his mouth tight, the way people do when they can't let themselves cry.

"Sir?"

"Thank you. For my wife and for—well, just thank you."

———

By the time I got back to Main, I only had a few moments left to do what had to be done. Aunt Ruby was right. Slinking was for the birds, no matter what happened when you stopped. I went up the library steps and pushed the tall creaking door open. Miss Prow sat behind her desk, gray and neat as always, except with her arm in a cast and her neck in a brace. And she wasn't even Levy or Caster or Finch, the last person anything should have happened to.

I waved for some reason, which was awkward. "Hey." My voice came out too small in the space between us.

"Hello, Ellie."

There was no use in working up to what I had to say. "I stopped by because I wanted to tell you—everything that happened—to you and—and everyone—that was me. Because of me." I wasn't sure if my jabbering made any sense whatsoever.

Miss Prow slipped a due date card in the book she'd been

reading as she felt around for an empty place on the desk and set the book down.

I couldn't read the expression on her face. "Maybe—maybe you already know that."

She reached under her desk and pulled out a box from the bakery next door. Then, still without a word, she stood stiffly, led the way to my usual table in the back, and lowered herself into a chair. I sat next to her, barely breathing, suspended between possibilities.

Up close, she'd worn thin as old paper. Her bent fingers worked at the box and finally got it open. Windmill cookies. "Sweep the crumbs into a napkin," she said. "And if someone comes in, everything goes under the table."

"Yes, Miss Prow. Of course." Of all the things I'd imagined she'd do, this wasn't one of them.

She ate three cookies, staring off into the distance, which might have been because of the brace, or because she couldn't stand to look at me. My one bite went down like sandpaper.

"Stale," she said, breaking the silence. "Small wonder. They've been there quite some time. But still—something sweet always jogs the brain." She rose to her feet and disappeared into the stacks.

Crumbs stuck to the back of my dry throat, and I was about to bolt for the water fountain when she came back around the corner, three books under her arm. *The Adventures of Sherlock Holmes. Emma.* And *The Great Norse Myths.*

"I think you've done enough nature study for the time being, don't you?" she said, patting my shoulder, which was all to say she'd forgiven me. But she didn't know everything, not yet.

I swallowed. "I broke into your house too." I pulled out her keys, clanked them down on the table. "And then I came here.

I didn't take anything—well, except a newspaper clipping, but—we—I had to. To know what to do."

She didn't answer for so long, I could hear the dust settling, which could only mean I'd just earned myself a trip straight back to the sheriff. Then her mouth twitched.

"I wondered where in heaven's name I'd put those keys," she remarked. "And who got my back window open. The thing wouldn't budge for thirty years."

"I can fix it," I offered quickly. "I'll get my dad to come with me."

Miss Prow tapped her fingers on the table. I'd be grounded for the rest of my life on top of everything else, but it didn't matter.

"I like a good cross breeze," she said, her mouth twitching again. "Let's leave it at that."

I would have hugged her, except for the brace. Instead, I pulled out the community service form and handed it to her. "I have ninety hours to do." I looked at her hopefully. "I can shelve, and I know where all the books are. If you'll let me come."

Miss Prow scanned the form, and her eyes lost their faded look. "I'll expect you tomorrow, then."

Over at the bakery, someone was making gingerbread and in that sudden flash of spicy- sweet, the knot that had been wrenching my stomach since I first saw the mark was gone, just like that.

34

I TIPTOED PAST THE SPECKLED
blue bowl and stuck a note under the griddle in case somebody
woke up before I got back. Then I shut the door on the kitchen's
Saturday morning warmth and stepped out to the sun meeting
the horizon, the taste of frost in the air.

The fields crackled with ice as I tramped up to my old entrance
into Oakbend Woods. I hadn't worked up the courage to come
this far before, and I wouldn't go in now—just see if I could face
it up close. But once I reached the familiar path, only bare trees
looked back, the pattern of their branches clear, nothing left to
hide. I filled my lungs with the clean pine straw smell, let it lift
me through a pink feathering of clouds all the way to the rising
sun. No more looking over my shoulder, no more dread of Curtis
or the Burning Tree. We were free, the empty woods and I.

I stood there so long that melting ice soaked up through my
sneakers, but I couldn't head home yet, not with hope pounding
through my veins, warming my face. The sun lit the woods,
prismed every frozen branch as I pulled Curtis's note from my
pocket, brushed off a few old pine needles, and unfolded it for
the millionth time.

I'll put in that good word.

Then I scooped up a handful of pebbles and ran, not stopping until I stood under Drew's window beneath the oaks that joined branches over his house. My first shot went short. Then a pebble pinged, and another, and the window jerked up. Drew stuck his head out, blinking sleep out of his eyes, wearing the gray T-shirt I'd given him a year ago. It was wrinkled and faded and about two sizes too small and the best thing I'd ever seen.

And I couldn't speak to save my life. This had been a mistake. I'd just shown my hand, told him everything. I wanted to run, but I couldn't do that either.

He didn't slam the window down, so whatever Curtis told him must have worked. "Hey," he said.

"Hi."

He combed his fingers through his hair. "Are you okay?"

"Yes. And you?" *And you.* Like we were at cotillion or something.

He swallowed a smile. "So, you're better? I mean your head?"

I shrugged. "It's still on. So, I guess that's good."

"Yeah, probably for the best."

This was going nowhere. My chilled feet had caught up to me, and I was shivering in spite of myself. I shoved my hands in my pockets to hide it. "So, your mom's okay?"

"She's great. It's like nothing happened."

"That's good." *Good.* Again. As if I only knew two words.

I scuffed my feet to scrape wet leaves from the bottoms of my shoes, my stomach turning over like I'd flipped cartwheels all around his yard. "I'm going to the woods this morning."

"Oh, really? Taking your notes again?"

"Actually, I thought I'd visit the Aspens."

"The sisters, huh?"

I'd forgotten he knew that group of trees.

"Just for a minute. Then we're having pancakes." Suddenly, I couldn't keep the words from tumbling out. "And after the fish fry this afternoon, everyone's coming to the bonfire at Grandad's."

"Sounds typical." He was smiling for real now, a glint in his blue eyes.

"Yeah. Would you—want to come?"

He disappeared from the window and the sash banged down. Maybe I'd gone too far, or he already had plans with Charlotte. A mourning dove cooed and cooed again, and I held my breath till his front door opened and he strode out, pulling on a navy jacket, holding his old red one out for me.

He'd come. And his coat still smelled like notebook paper when I zipped it up.

"You're really here, right?" he said, looking down at me like he couldn't believe it. "I would have come by before, but you told me not to. And I—I wasn't sure you'd want to talk to me again."

"I do if you do."

He smiled, the one I'd known all my life. "That's the pact." Then he reached over and straightened my collar, and his fingers brushed my skin. The warmth in his eyes sent me floating. This was going to be okay. More than okay. It was going to be brilliant.

"Come on, then," I said, and we walked together to the bright sunlit woods.

THE END

ACKNOWLEDGMENTS

When I was ten, my grandad paid me one dollar a page for what turned out to be an extremely long story (I see you, Dickens). He framed the first dollar and called me an author. So thank you, James Riley, for valuing what I loved to do from the very beginning.

That early project also had a coauthor, which taught me that writing isn't done in a vacuum (literal or metaphorical). Stories need others to survive, and that is absolutely true of the book you're holding in your hands.

The members of the DFW Writers Workshop provided weekly critique and encouragement and basically kept me from writing chapters of scenery with no plot. Thanks in particular to Brooke Fossey, Lauren Danhof, J.B. Sanders, Jr., Brian Tracey, and Rosemary Clement, who helped me find my blind spots and also affirmed what was working. A HUGE thanks to my beta readers from the workshop: A. Lee Martinez, who understood my vision for the story and whose comments always drove my writing closer to that vision; Leslie Lutz, who sharpened both my scenes and my sentences; and John Bartell, whose superpower is knowing when and how to end a scene.

Thank you to Milli Jacks, Susan Banner, Maurisa Riley, and

Diana Cullum, who read early drafts of this book (sometimes multiple times). Your feedback made the story stronger. To Sarah Kay Ndjerareou and the Art House Dallas Awaken Creativity Group, thank you for your consistent encouragement throughout the process of bringing this work of imagination to the page. And to Sandra Fernandez Rhoads, thank you, thank you, thank you for reading the first draft of this manuscript, for the many deep (and also hilarious) brainstorming sessions, and most of all, for believing in the story's potential.

To Steve Laube, thank you for giving this book a home at Enclave. Lisa Laube, your editing finesse brought the story structure alive. Thank you also to Trissina, Lindsay, Sara Ella, Coralie, and the entire Enclave team for making this journey rewarding. Because of you, I never felt I was walking it alone. Lyndsey Lewellen, the cover is gorgeous and exactly right, beyond what I could have imagined.

And to my family, who made it all possible. Mom, this book literally would not have been written without the many hours you gave me time to write. Thank you for listening to my stories over the years . . . the multitudes of them . . . for all the read-alouds, and for the thousand trips to the library that shaped my imaginative world. Dad, I think it must have been your Flying Unicorn stories that sparked it all. Who could have known where those fantastical adventures would lead? All my life, you showed me what courage means. Thank you for always encouraging me to take the right adventure, no matter the cost.

To my kids–Joseph, thank you for being this book's first reader and for your insightful questions that helped build this story world. Riley, your enthusiasm and inquisitiveness have expanded my brain and creativity in all directions. Emily, your many notes of encouragement inspired me, time and time again, to keep going. I love you all tons.

And to my husband, Jonathan, *thank you* is simply not enough for all the hours you held down the fort, or provided critique, or simply listened (and listened and listened). I could not have gone out on this creative limb, could not have failed and then tried again, without you. Me and you. That's the pact. And it's going to be brilliant.

ABOUT THE AUTHOR

Helen Dent's career as a writer began at age nine, when her grandfather paid her a dollar a page for what turned into quite a lengthy story. She studied monster theory (among other things) in graduate school, taught English at a Chinese university, and toured the Scottish Hebrides in a car with a needy radiator. Now she lives in Texas with her husband, kids, a cat, and a hamster. She belongs to the DFW Writers Workshop, the Fort Worth Poetry Society, and Art House Dallas.